The Wash

A Novella

Dragonfly Publishing

LISA WOLSTENHOLME

Second Edition Published December 2021
Copyright © 2020 Lisa Wolstenholme

This is a work of fiction. Names, characters, businesses, places, events and incidents are either the products of the author's imagination or used in a fictitious manner. Any resemblance to actual persons, living or dead, or actual events is purely coincidental.

Because of the dynamic nature of the Internet, any web addresses or links contained in this book may have changed since publication and may no longer be valid. The views expressed in this work are solely those of the author and do not necessarily reflect the views of the publisher and the publisher hereby disclaims any responsibility for them.

National Library of Australia
Cataloguing-in-Publication data:
                        The Wash/fiction

ISBN: (sc) 978-0-6453505-1-7
general – fiction

For Mark

Because you are the best fish in the sea.

April 2003 – Losing Jake

Mum's face is ghostly white as we enter the room, the smell of Pine O Clean invading my nostrils. She falters as we reach the slab and stumbles, falling against Dad.

A man dressed in blue scrubs, his brow furrowed, pulls back the white sheet. 'Ready?'

Dad nods, closing his eyes as if not daring to look.

I stand transfixed. *It's not him. This is a mistake.* Hold my breath as the sheet is folded one-fifth down and a face appears.

'His face is ... it's grey?' I gasp.

'Oh my god.' Dad's voice cracks and he pulls Mum into his chest as a wail escapes her.

I am numb. My mouth won't move, my chest static, eyes fixed on the alien-like face, its eyelids closed, lips blue. Whitened blotches cover the cheeks, nose and mouth, each one a messy peak with holes.

Nausea rises from deep in my gut, my throat constricting.

No. Jake—no! You stupid idiot! No!

Mum and Dad sob into each other as the doctor places his hand on my dad's shoulder. Dad looks up briefly, nods, then buries his head in Mum's hair.

It's been a week since we identified Jake's body. At least, I think it has. Time seems to have stopped, every day melding in one gigantic piece of shit. I am sick of hearing, 'sorry for your loss,' fed up with the pity looks, frustrated at the embargo on talking about why Jake is now dead.

His funeral is two days before my sixteenth birthday. Some fucking birthday that's going to be. The mention of a party makes me want to vomit. The thought of smiles and presents and cake at a time like this ...

It's not like Jake had been a huge part of my life of late. Too busy getting pissed and doing god-knows-what with the low life's he hung around with. So much for the shining star of a brother and son, and I'm sure our parents didn't expect him to end like this—death by misadventure. He had more booze and heroin in his system than blood, I suspect, and the term 'suicide' has been whispered on more than one occasion. So where are his so-called mates now? Will they come to his funeral and accept their part in it? And what was he doing on the beach anyway? Why wasn't one of them with him?

If they do come, I will spit on each of their faces, disgusting runts.

I often think about the guy who found him—a surfer, I think, out to catch a morning wave—and how he must have felt discovering Jake's body lying face down in the wash on Scarborough beach. I don't know what I'd have done in that situation. Thrown-up, probably. I wonder whether he thinks about Jake, is curious to know what happened to him, or just wants to forget the whole sorry episode and try to get on with his life? Would it have left psychological scars? Would he now need to see a Psych? Mum did say she wanted to meet the poor guy and thank him for alerting the police, but what else was he supposed to do? Just leave a bloated, grey body bobbing along the sand as if it were a dead fish? But I guess there's no etiquette for this sort of thing, you just have to wing it and hope you've handled it the right way.

See Jake? See what a mess you've left behind!

~~~

'Clara—' Mum's voice carries. 'It's time to go.'

I can't move ... my chest constricts and nausea grips.

This can't be happening. It's not right. It's a mistake. Jake'll be home soon.

Voices mumble from the lounge room, my cue to get my shoes on and head out to the waiting hearse. Mum and Dad are already seated inside when I reach it. A big, black beast with large windows, darkened at the front, crystal clear at the back so everyone can see the jarrah coffin inside. Flowers flanking its sides and top; white carnations in the shape of 'Son', lilies in a bouquet on top, a heart of red roses with 'Brother' in the centre.

My legs buckle and I tumble against the rear passenger door. Mum shoots me a quizzical look and Dad pushes open the door so I can clamber in.

'You okay, love?' he asks, reaching for my hand.

I nod, buckle up my belt, eyes fixed forward. I don't want to know what's behind me. Don't want to *feel* anything.

The journey to Scarborough Baptist Church is thankfully short—in the same suburb as our home in Doubleview, but the hearse travels so slowly it feels like the journey will go on forever, and even though the chilly ocean breeze has signalled that autumn is in full swing, I open the window, holding my breath until fresher air can fill my lungs and the stale constricting cabin of this beast we ride in.

We pull up outside a church that looks more like a primary school with its blue feature wall and small playpark and get out as if we are walking in treacle. Several cars pull up behind and an array of friends and family get out and walk over to us, each face frowning or wearing a feeble smile. After moments of quiet words and occasional sobs, all faces seem to blur into one. I want to flee. Find a quiet nook where I can hide from the well-wishers and do-gooders offering, 'it'll get better with time.' What the fuck is that supposed to mean, anyway?

~~~

'I'd like to invite Clara Reid, Jake's sister, to come up and read for us.' The priest nods at me pulling me into the present, but I freeze. I have nothing prepared, nothing written about how much I loved my brother, how much I'll miss him.

Members of the congregation all stare in unison, but I can't catch my breath, can't seem to raise my weary torso off the pew. An uncomfortable silence ensues.

The priest coughs. 'Perhaps Jake's cousin, Leona, will come up and read from the book of Wisdom 4:7–

15 Untarnished life, this is ripe old age.'

Leona makes her way up to the pulpit, places a piece of paper on it and between snuffles, reads the passage. I close my eyes to listen.

'... for the fascination of evil throws good things into the shade, and the whirlwind of desire corrupts a simple heart,' she says.

I glare over at my parents, shaking my head. *Did they choose this?* But they are in the throes of their grief, and words, misplaced or otherwise, are there to comfort them in the hopes that Jake will be moving on to a better place. Ironic.

~~~

Jake's coffin is lowered slowly into the ground, the priest reciting, '... and we commit his body to the ground, earth to earth, ashes to ashes, dust to dust. And we beseech thine infinite goodness to give us grace to live in thy fear and love and to die in thy favour, that when the judgment shall come which thou hast committed to thy well-beloved Son, both this our brother and we may be found acceptable in thy sight. Grant this, O merciful Father, for the sake of Jesus Christ, our only Saviour, Mediator, and Advocate. Amen.'

No 'Amen' leaves my lips. I am sickened by these words. My already waning faith has now reached non-existence as my mum and dad cling desperately to theirs.

Tiff and Flick stand either side of me, squeezing my hands as the last interments are spoken. Still no tears fall, just insidious anger bubbling away inside, threatening to erupt. The cooling Freo doctor chills my bones and all I want to do is run, get as far away from this excruciating event as possible. I turn to Flick. 'Can we get out of here?'

Flick nods, her eyes glistening, and we step back and walk away from Jake's graveside. My parents don't notice, drowning in their own sorrows.

The further away we get, the more gulps of air I take in as if breathing for the first time.

'You okay?' Tiff says, stopping and pulling me to her.

'Fine. Just needed air.' I am stone in her arms.

Flick strokes my hair, shushing, her arms wrapping around us both. 'We're here for you,' she says.

We eventually head back to the cemetery as people are leaving Jake's graveside, heading off to the wake being held at the Lifesavers Club where Jake used to be a volunteer. Christ, another few hours of unbearable politeness and offers of sympathy and, 'if you need anything ...' I just want to be on my own.

~~~

Mum taps my shoulder. I turn and stare into her blotchy face streaked by so many tears. 'Clara—' she grabs me and sobs. I hold on for a few minutes, still no words to say, until Dad strokes my arm and says, 'We're going to the wake now.' I pull away and nod, tossing a glance at Flick and Tiff, who both look as sombre as I feel.

Dad holds my hand throughout the silent car journey, each of us too deep in our own miseries to find the energy for small talk. When we pull up at the club, people are already assembled out front, waiting for us to arrive as if it's a wedding and not a funeral.

Inside, I regroup with my friends. Tiff has already scored a drink from a gullible-looking barman after flashing her fake Smartrider, and skulls it like her life depended on it.

'I'll see if I can get us a bottle,' she says, and well ... succeeds and we spend the next few hours on a wall overlooking the beach, the three of us getting steadily pissed.

'I wonder where he was found,' Tiff says.

I glare at her.

'I don't think we should think about it,' Flick says, scowling at Tiff. Tiff shakes her head and glugs the last dregs of wine.

'We should get back,' I say, clambering off the walk. But as I try to walk, my legs buckle and I stumble forwards, grazing my hands against warm concrete. 'Dammit!' I'd rather liked the numbing effect of alcohol, but now reality bites and my palms sting.

'Clara—' Flick jumps down from the wall and heaves me up. 'You okay, hun?' she scrutinises my face, brows furrowed, mouth agape.

Rubbing my hands against my skirt, I reply, 'I'm okay. Thanks.'

The briefest moments of escapism passed; we walk back to the club trudging as if trying to delay the inevitable.

'What happened?' My Dad rushes towards me and

grabs my shoulders.

'I fell ...' is all I can muster.

He sniffs close to my mouth. 'Have you been ... drinking?'

I glance at the other two and drop my head.

'Clara—*why*?'

'I'm sorry,' I mutter, then peek up at him.

He shakes his head. 'So, you're following in Jake's footsteps now?'

'No!'

'Get a grip, Clara. For God's sake.' He turns away from me as shame engulfs.

Late-April 2003

Being sixteen doesn't suit me, well ... not now. Mentally, I feel like I should be much older, but not necessarily wiser. Cards lined up on top of the mantle tell me I'm sixteen, but are interspersed with sympathy cards announcing, 'sorry for your loss'. There is nothing special about today.

My party dress hangs from the top of the lounge room door, freshly ironed by Mum. My family have decided that my celebration of coming-of-age is still going ahead even though I have told them many times I cannot rejoice in this day, or any other for that matter. I feel lost, my life in hiatus as thoughts still swirl in gay abandon making day-to-day living seem unreachable. But I have promised my parents I will go to the party, be the gracious daughter, play the part of blossoming teenager, even though it will all be a pretence. It is an act for them, for others, so they can believe that the world is still spinning as it should.

~~~

Jake's room seems so cold. The strong smell of Brut aftershave no longer lingers and there are coffee cup stains on his bedside table from the last time he was home. I sit on the bed, reach underneath and pull out his diary, idly flicking through the pages. Most are bare, but occasionally a birthday note, anniversary, or special event are written in. My birthday is circled, stars around it. A few days before a scrawl reading, 'Buy Clara's present,' in thick black pen. *What was he going to get me? A book perhaps?* I kneel down beside the bed and pat underneath, searching. But nothing except socks, magazines and fluff is there.

If he had bought me the book I wanted, we'd have both read it and spent hours discussing the ins-and-outs of the plot, characters, arc, writing style. Jake and I shared a passion for books. We both liked historical fiction and Jake was championing my desire to be a writer of some sort. We'd write together too: short stories, poems, made-up newspaper articles—and scrutinise every word, every detail. And when Jake was treading the path that eventually led to his demise, I wrote him letter-after-letter telling him how much I missed him, loved him, wanted to support him. He only ever replied to a few. I guess some roads are one-way.

I get up and notice an envelope on his bedside table. Curiosity gets the better of me and I grab it and pull out a letter.

20/11/02

Clara,

I know you mean well, but you have to respect my choices. I never once said I didn't love you, or Mum and Dad, it's just that you're all suffocating me and not letting me find my own way in life. That's why I had to leave.

I know you don't agree with what I'm doing, but I'm sure it's just something I have to go through to experience life to the fullest. I wish you could understand that. When you get to uni you'll know what it's like—the pressure to fit in and be part of the social scene—and how easy it can be to get into bad habits (your words, not mine).

Please Clara, understand that I will do my best to be there for you when you need me, as I know you will for me, but you need to let go of the reins a little and let me enjoy life.

I'll see you all at Christmas. Until then, be good to yourself and tell the oldies I love them.

Jake

Why did he never give this to me?

A sigh escapes me, and I fold the paper and stuff it back into the envelope. But he's right ... I don't understand. I can't comprehend how having a good time can so quickly become an addiction to drugs and alcohol. Which friends made him take these things? Who was responsible for offering the first swig or toke?

None of it matters now, though. Jake is dead, my parents are heartbroken, and his so-called friends don't seem to give a shit.

～～～

Silence fills the car as we drive to the Scarborough Beach Bar, the venue for my party. Mum holds a cake box on her lap, tutting at Dad every time he takes a corner too quickly or goes over a speed bump too fast. I suspect they feel as hesitant as I do about tonight, as if we've all read the same guide that says we must smile and be seen to be enjoying ourselves.

Dad pulls up into the car park and lets out a sigh. 'Ready?'

No, not really.

Mum nods and Dad gets out and helps her out. She scowls as he grabs the box.

We make our way inside, passing by the round marble bar with glasses hanging like fairy lights from a brass rack above and up to the function area overlooking the pool. Cheers erupt as I enter, the space filled with friends and family all hell-bent on having a good time. I spy Flick and make a beeline for her.

She smiles as I approach and reaches out for a hug. 'You okay?' she whispers.

I nod, plastering a faux grin on my face as people come up to wish me well.

A table at the back is already filling up with presents of various sizes. I glance over them looking for book-shaped ones, hoping for a gem to enable me to escape my shit life for a few hours. I look over at my parents. Mum already has a glass of wine in hand and I secretly wish I could do the same, gulping as Dad's voice echoes through my mind: *So, you're following in Jake's footsteps now?*

Anna, Tiffany and Stella are huddled in a corner and turn in unison to look at me, each tossing a meek 'hello' as Flick and I walk over.

'How you going?' Anna asks, frowning. 'This must be weird for you.'

I nod. 'I'm going to make the most of it. I mean, you only turn sixteen once.' I smile, hoping to ease the palpable tension thickening the air between us.

Music blares from speakers housed either side of the venue. Pop tunes signal awkward movements and shuffles as we all wonder whether or not to dance. *Am I expected to?*

'You brought ... you know?' I ask Tiff.

She reaches into her bag and pulls out a stainless-steel water bottle. She jerks her head to the side, and we all follow in silence towards the lady's bathroom.

Once inside, we take turns to glug the liquid in the bottle—it could be vodka, I'm not sure—each pulling faces as the bitter liquid hits our tongues. We stare at each, no one quite knowing what to say next. I bite the bullet. 'Girls, I think it's time to party,' and nod towards the door, taking a deep breath as we trundle out, drawing on what little is left of my energy.

<hr/>

The Book Thief lies on my bedside table and I reach over to grab it, opening it up at the first page to read the inscription:

> *Jake said you wanted this for your birthday, so this is with love from him.*
>
> *Mum & Dad x*

A sob escapes me, and I hurl the book across the room and bury myself in my doona. He should've been here to give me it.

May 2003

My parents have arranged for me to see to the school counsellor, assuming I need to have someone to talk to about my grief—or lack of it.

Mr Davies opens his office door and beckons me in. 'Good morning, Clara. Please take a seat.'

I sit down in the chair opposite him, a typical IKEA Poäng—not very comfortable as I'm forced backwards, bouncing. 'Hello,' I say, glancing around the room: a brick-exposed office with minimal furnishings.

'So your parents have asked me to talk to you about how you're feeling since you lost your brother, but before we talk, I need to let you know that this is a safe space for you. What we say in here, stays in here. Okay?'

'Why?'

'Sorry?' His brows furrow into a monobrow.

'Why have they asked you?'

'Well ... I think they're concerned about you.'

'Concerned how?'

'About how you're dealing with the loss of your brother. They feel like you're shutting yourself off from them.'

'Oh.' I wrap my arms across my stomach and lean

forward, still trying to get comfortable. 'Guess I'm still numb.'

He nods. 'I understand it's been over a month since he died. How have you been?'

'Fine.'

'It must've been a challenging time for you. Have you been able to talk to anyone about it?'

'Don't really want to think about it, to be honest.'

'Does it feel bad to think about it?'

What kind of a stupid question is that? 'What do you reckon?'

'Is it helpful to not think about it?'

I nod, twisting my chestnut plait as butterflies rave in my gut.

We sit in silence for a few moments. Mr Davies— Alan as he wants me to call him—scribbles something down on a notepad in his lap.

'What are you writing?' I ask.

'Just a few notes for me to refer back to.'

'What do they say?'

He draws in a deep breath. 'That I think you may be struggling coming to terms with Jake's death. That you may be in denial.'

Huh? 'Why would I be in denial? I know he's dead. I know he's not coming back.' I bite my lip.

'Perhaps denial is the wrong word. What do you think would be a better word to describe where you're at?' His voice is soft, soothing almost.

'I dunno, I'm not a counsellor!' I glare at him. But moments pass and I feel bad for my outburst. "Sorry—I ... I guess I'm still feeling *raw*?'

'Raw. I'll make a note,' he says, scribbling. When he's finished, he looks over at me, but doesn't speak. It makes me feel uneasy.

'How long does this last?' I ask, tugging more forcibly at my hair.

'About fifty minutes. Are you worried about getting to your class on time?'

'Maybe ...'

'You seem uncomfortable, Clara. Do you want to share with me what you're thinking?'

I shake my head. 'Not really.'

He scribbles again, and it starts to irritate me. I fidget in the seat, letting go of my hair and picking at a cotton tag on my school skirt.

'How's school going?'

'It's fine, really. I'm fine—just don't want to talk about what's happened.'

'Okay, but I need to make sure you have everything you need to make school bearable. You're what ... year 10 now? Soon be time to pick your Tertiary Entrance Exam subjects.'

'Uh-huh.'

'Know what you want to do?'

My gut pangs. *I know what I want to do, it's just ...*

'Clara?'

'Yes?' My eyes dart back in his direction. 'Oh ... err ... sorry.'

'So, aspirations?'

My pulse starts to race. 'I ... I—' The words won't come out. I flush as blood pumps at fifteen bar pressure through my veins.

Alan pours a glass of water and holds it out to me. I grab it and gulp the liquid, hoping the tightness around my neck will ease.

'Are you okay?'

'Think so,' I reply, finally finding my voice again. 'Don't know what that was about.' I glance at my knees, a feeling of shame washing over me. 'Sorry.'

'It's okay, Clara. Honestly.'

And clear as mud, the words, 'I don't know what I want to do yet,' pop out of my mouth. Except they're not true—I did know, only ...

'Well, if you need any help with picking subjects, let me know.'

'Thanks.' I feign a smile.

Silence ensues and my mind races. *What does he want me to say?* The fan on his computer whirs.

After a long period of me picking skirt fluff and Alan sitting quietly, occasionally smiling across at me, he finally breaks the silence. 'I think it'd be good for you to come and see me each week ... just for a while, to check in and let me know how you're going. What d'ya reckon?'

'Will that ease my parent's minds?'

He chuckles. 'I guess it might.'

'Okay then.' *Anything to keep them off my back.*

'Good. Come and see me next Wednesday. I'm free at 2pm, okay?'

'I need to check my timetable.'

'Um ... I already did. You have Sport.'

'You can do that?'

He nods.

'Then I guess it's okay.'

'I'll send you an email reminder. So, see you next week.'

'Uh-huh. See you next week.' I get up and leave, my mind reeling from realising every member of staff has free reign on my student file. *Surely that's an invasion of privacy?*

My mood is rock-bottom as I make my way to my French class, worsened by knowing that I'll be stared at, probably gossiped about, for walking in late.

～～～

'Clara—dinner.' Mum yells from the kitchen.

She smiles up at me as I reach the table.

'I've made your favourite—Soutzoukakia,' she says, placing bowls of rice and meatballs in the centre of the table.

'Thanks Mum.' But my heart's not in it. After being ensconced in homework for several hours and having

18

an appetite akin to that of a mouse, the thought of a hefty dose of meat and rice leaves me cold. I plop a few spoonful's onto my plate and manage a couple of mouthfuls.

'Well?'

'It's great. Thanks.'

My Dad eyes me and mumbles to Mum, 'Guess she's still on a diet.'

'I'm not on a diet!' I snap. 'I'm just not hungry!'

He scowls and turns to Mum. 'It's delicious, darling.'

We eat in silence, save for the clinking of cutlery against the fine bone china plates, and it doesn't take long for my measly portion to disappear.

When my parents have both finished, I get up to leave.

'Clara, before you go—' Dad says, 'did you see the Counsellor today?'

'You know I did.'

'Well, how did it go?'

'It was fine. I'm surprised he hasn't told you already.' I can't contain the sarcasm.

'What do you mean?'

'I thought Big Brother would've reported back by now.'

'That's not what it's about, darling—'

'What is it about then?'

Mum reaches over and takes my hand. 'We're

worried about you and thought perhaps the school counsellor could help you talk about what's happened, so you can deal with it better.' She squeezes my hand and her eyes turn watery.

'Deal with what? Jake dying? How is anyone supposed to deal with that, for fuck's sake?' My anger bubbles.

'Clara! There's no need for that kind of language. We're just trying to help.' Dad's tone raises an octave.

'I don't need your help. I just want to get on with my life.'

'I know, darling, we're trying to do the same. It's—' Mum's voice cracks and she looks away.

'It's hard for us too, you know,' Dad says, completing her sentence.

I shuffle around, unsure of what to say.

'Clara—please, just try not to bottle it all up otherwise you won't get over it all.'

'But how are we supposed to get over it? I—' Tears well, but I gulp them back. 'I just don't want to talk about it, okay?'

Dad's head drops and he sighs. 'Okay. But we're here if you do want to talk.'

'I know.'

I'm about to walk away when Mum says, 'Clara … there's something else we need to discuss with you.'

Frowning, I turn around. 'What is it?'

'Jake's room—' Dad's voice wavers and he reaches

for Mum's hand. 'We think it's time we went through it.'

'And do what?'

'Clear out some of his stuff ... clothes, knick-knacks, you know.'

'Why would you do that?' My fists clench.

'Because it breaks my heart having it all there as a constant reminder,' Mum yells before collapsing into my dad, sobbing.

'We need to do this Clara, for all our sakes. We need to let some of what Jake was go,' Dad says.

'But ... I can't. I don't want to.'

'Our therapist says we need to clear it out, freshen it up and turn it into something new, something we can all live with.'

'No! I won't. You can't do that!'

'Please Clara—we need to do this. We're grieving too, for Christ's sake. Don't you think it's been the worst time in our lives too?'

I stand transfixed, anger and shame intertwining. 'But why now? Isn't it too soon?'

Dad gently moves away from Mum and comes over towards me, wrapping me in his arms. 'There'll never be a good time, sweetheart, but we have to get through this.'

Even though being in my father's arms has always felt like the safest place in the world, and has been a sanctuary during bad times, right now, all I feel is ... numb.

～～～

Jake's bedroom is blanketed in a thin layer of dust. I don't think it's been cleaned since he left for uni and moved in with his mates. I guess it's the last thing anyone wants to do now.

I sit idly on his bed, scrutinising every surface, every nook. My eyes fall on his bookcase overloaded with novels, how-to guides and travel booklets. I've read most of them. Jake and I were like a tag-team—we'd take it in turns to buy a book and read it, then pass it on to each other. After we'd both read something, we'd spend ages discussing it, like our own little book club. Occasionally, Jake would indulge in trashy works just to provoke a heated debate, but we always seemed to be on the same page with most of our critiques.

Jake was the one who championed my writing cause the most. One of my earliest memories was of him handing me paper and an electric blue Sharpie—I'd felt so grown up holding it in my hand—and telling me to write him a story and draw some pictures. As a five-year-old, I was so excited to do it, especially since Jake sat with me and we talked through the plot, who my characters were, and what they would be doing. From that moment onwards, Jake and I had a bond so strong that my mum would often say we were two halves of the same soul.

Memories flood my mind, but no tears fall.

Why can't I cry?

I spend the next few hours sitting on the floor next to his bookcase, poring over the books, reminiscing about discussions we've had. Each one holds a memory

I can't bear to let go of. Happy times, before Jake started university and fell in with the wrong crowd.

Once the bookcase has been dealt with, I make a start on his wardrobe rifling through boxes of comics, more books, his treasured collection of Marvel figurines, clothes and shoes. As I pull out belongings, I find a brown paper wrapped package underneath a pile of belts. It has my name on it and I already know what it is. I tear at the wrapping to reveal the book, the one I wanted. An inscription on the first page reads:

Sis,

Enjoy! Can't wait to review it with you.

Much love,

Jake x

Trembling and struggling to breathe, I draw it to my chest.

July 2003

'How have you been this week, Clara?' Alan asks as I sit legs-crossed in the bouncy chair.

'I'm okay. It was good to have a break for a couple of weeks.'

'Go anywhere nice?'

'Camping in Kalbarri. Much warmer than Perth.'

Alan grins and tops up his glass of water. 'What'd you do up there?'

'Read, mostly.'

'Written anything yet?'

I shake my head. 'Just can't seem to ... ' A wave of sadness washes over me.

'It'll take time.'

'I know.'

I've been coming to these weekly sessions for several months now, and honestly, I'm starting to feel a bit more human. Alan has been talking me through the grieving steps and I now realise that the anger I've been holding onto—towards Jake, my parents, but mostly myself—has been stopping me from moving on. He's been guiding me through being more present, more focused on each day. Sometimes it feels as though I'm putting off the inevitable breakdown, but for now, day-by-day, life is bearable.

But my writing is at an impasse; I just don't want to do it, can't do it. Every time I try, I get nauseous and my heart races. It's as if putting pen to paper is somehow disrespectful to Jake because of the passion we shared for it and I'm in a state of flux, not quite knowing what I'm supposed to do now.

In spite of all that's come to pass, something else has grown inside me—a curiosity perhaps to uncover the inner workings of the mind—my mind, Jake's mind. I want—no, *need* to understand why Jake trod the path he did, and after each session with Alan, find myself longing for a deeper understanding, contemplating the idea that maybe I'm supposed to find out.

'So, have you given any more thought to next years' subjects?'

I'm jolted back from my musings. 'Um ... not really.'

'You mentioned a few weeks back that your career choice might've changed. Is that still the case?'

'Uh-huh.'

'Want to talk about it?'

I pause, searching my mind for a response that won't close off the topic. 'Perhaps ...'

Alan's eyes lock with mine and he raises his eyebrows as if anticipating a revelation.

'Well ... it's just that, as you know, I'd always wanted to be a writer, a novelist or journalist perhaps, but now I seem incapable of writing, so it's kind of gone to shit.'

'Frustrating, huh, and I guess the pressure's on to pick your subjects for next year.'

'Feels that way.'

'Still thinking of going to university?'

I nod. 'Just don't know which direction to go in, although—' I take a deep breath, 'I'm getting more and more interested in learning about how our minds tick.'

'You're thinking about psychology?' He raises his brows.

'Possibly ...'

'And this is something you could see yourself doing for work?'

'It's probably a stupid idea, but I keep coming back to it.'

Alan leans forward as if he's about to reveal pearls of wisdom no one else can be privy to. 'Well ... looking at your reports, past grades, you've got the brains for it—pardon the pun,' he chuckles, '—but I wonder if the motives behind following this kind of career path are because you genuinely want to work in this field, or because you need to know what happened to Jake.'

'Um ... both, probably.'

'Your writing—do you hope it's something you'll come back to?'

I frown. 'Not sure. Kinda feels like it's all wrong for me now.'

'Wrong?'

'Yeah. Like I can't do it anymore because Jake's not

here. Not sure if that's something I'll ever get over.'

Alan nods his head. 'Seems like writing is intrinsically linked to Jake, and because there is no Jake, the writing has disappeared too?'

'Guess so,' I reply glumly.

'And how do you feel about that?'

'Sad. Like a lifelong dream has ended.'

'How would you feel if we focused on understanding the link between Jake and your writing? We might be able to find a way to untether them.'

'I don't know. It just feels—'

'Too soon?'

'Yeah. Too soon.'

'Okay, let's park it for now. We can always come back to it later, when you feel ready, okay?'

'Okay.'

'So times up, Clara. I'll see you next week.'

'Yep ... thanks. See you next week.'

~~~

I've been staring at the same form for hours, contemplating. Every now and again I put a tick next to a subject, then rub it out. The paper is covered with traces of pencil and bits of eraser.

This is too hard, the pressure bubbling to get it done, handed in, or I may not get my subjects of choice.

Mulling over my last conversation with Alan, my pencil hovers over English Literature. Before Jake died,

I would have ticked it in a heartbeat, so convinced I was of my way forward, but now my pencil is poised, but not ready to commit.

I scan over the list of subjects again trying to figure out which would be the most useful to get me into uni, but I'm clueless—haven't researched courses, let alone entry requirements—so figure I need to get online and look up undergraduate courses to at least get an idea of direction.

~~~~~

Jake's voice tells me to weigh up the pros and cons of each option to help figure out which is the best choice for me. But another voice, higher in tone and smaller in impact, as if it belongs to a child, keeps calling out: *But why did you die, Jake?*

I can't ignore it. I need to understand what happened and as this thought circles, I am drawn to the words now displayed on my computer screen: 'Bachelor of Arts (Psychology and Addiction Studies)'. *That's it!* Immediately, I scan the entry requirements and look at my subject listings. The fuzziness in my head clears and I tick all the subjects that satisfy them, plus a few others I know I actually enjoy. And just like that the task is complete and I feel lighter, the errant thoughts now quieted.

Like a hermit emerging from a cave, I leave my room and head towards the kitchen for some food. As the bedroom door closes behind me, one final freeing thought blares: *I never have to write again.*

February 2006

The university campus is huge: grey concrete buildings rising out of the ground, pathways squirreling between them creating a maze. My head spins as I try and position myself, searching memories of my orientation day to figure out where I need to be. My only comfort is that Anna is studying a Marketing, Advertising and Public Relations undergraduate course here, so I'm not completely alone. Not that being on my own is something I struggle with anymore.

I float through the morning like a zombie as reams of information are thrown at me: subject info, campus details, book lists—an endless stream. By lunchtime I am tired, disjointed, and overloaded. I text Anna to find out if she's free. Thankfully, a response soon arrives, and we arrange to meet in one of the many cafés littered around the site.

'The food's nice and cheap,' Anna says, sipping a latte. 'At least we'll be able to afford to eat.'

We both titter.

'Except I've a squillion books to buy, and they're not cheap!' I show Anna my list and she tuts. 'Think I might need to a get a part-time job to see me through.'

'You should come and work at Maccas with me!' She says squealing.

I wrinkle my nose. 'I've heard the pay is shit.'

'Yeah ... but it's something, at least.'

I contemplate her idea as I sip my coffee and munch on a double-choc muffin, imagining myself in the uniform, smiling and being faux-friendly to customers. *Would you like fries with that, sir?*

'Nah. I'm not the most person-centred of people.'

'Already using the lingo, eh?' Anna raises her eyebrows at me. 'We'll have to start calling you straight-jacket.'

I snort. 'Maybe you can be my first patient.'

Anna scowls and sips her coffee.

We chat for a while until the next phase of today's uni life beckons, hug and go our separate ways. But as I head towards the hall for my next lecture, my gut twists in protest. *This is what I want, isn't it?*

~~~

'How was your first day?' Mum asks while spooning mash into a bowl in the centre of the table.

'Good.'

She drops a spoon in the bowl with a heavy clang as if making a point.

'A lot to take in,' I say, hoping to appease.

'It'll get easier ... once you've got a routine going.' She continues laying out the food. 'Did you think about our offer of a car?'

I shake my head. 'The bus is fine; besides, I can't afford the insurance.'

'We can help with that,' my dad pipes up, 'at least until you get a job.'

'Not sure what my timetable's going to be like yet, so can't get a job until I know what I'm doing.'

'Fair enough. The offer's there if you want it.'

A toss Dad a smile and dish up some dinner.

Something about working, about driving—it all feels too grown up, too ... responsible. I'm not sure I feel ready for it. Silently, I resolve to take one day at a time, as Alan kept telling me back at school.

~~~~~

The routine of university life is comforting and consistent, and for the first time since Jake died, I feel a glimmer of hope that there could be more to my life than living in the shadow of my lost brother. But lurking in the back of my mind is one prominent thought: I *will* find out why. It's my driving force, the only thing that keeps the propellers turning.

My favourite subject so far is Addiction Studies Fundamentals. I seem to inhale the subject matter as if needing to fill my brain with every piece of Jake's puzzle. It's the only one mildly scratching the itch.

Wednesday mornings are catch-up time with Anna. We have claimed a bench underneath a red gum as our own, where we sit with a coffee and chat for an hour. Anna is loving her course—she's always wanted to be a Public Relations exec and has a clear five-year plan to make that dream a reality. Sometimes I feel like I should be planning my future in a similar fashion, but my 'one day at a time' mantra holds firm, ensuring I don't get too ahead of myself. *Why is that?*

'Hey,' Anna says, straightening. 'We haven't had a girl's night out for ages.'

'Yeah … I know.'

'Let's do Saturday night.' Anna busies herself with texting Flick, Tiff and Stella, and within seconds her phone emits a series of pings. 'It's a goer,' she announces. 'We can do pre-drinkies at my place then get a taxi into Northbridge.'

I frown, not sure I'm up for a night of drinking and dancing.

'Clara—we're doing this.' She scowls at me, her eyebrows arching almost to her bleached blond hairline.

'But—' I try to come up with a smart retort, but my mind is blank. Truth is, I've been avoiding social gatherings, the temptation to guzzle away my woes is too easy, and I don't want to end up like Jake.

~~~

Flick links my arm to steady us both as we head into another bar. I am tipsy, my resolve to go easy on the alcohol having fallen by the wayside. All five of us have thrown caution to the wind and overindulged. At this point in time only Tiff has a partner, the rest of us prowling—checking out potential suitors through our beer goggles. I like this heady feeling of not quite being present, of feeling invincible, of not giving a shit about everyday life. The only problem is, when I catch a taste of it, I don't want it to end, and so for the rest of the night my mantra reigns supreme. For now, I am living.

Stella's feet won't keep still—she's itching to dance. A silent agreement is made, and we all drink up and make our way out of the bar and on towards the nearest nightclub.

Music pounds in my ears, vibrating through my body like I'm on one of those machines with a strap around my butt trying to shake off excess flab. Stella, Tiff and Anna don't bother with drinks and head straight for the dancefloor, suspiciously close to a group of guys as Rhianna's *S.O.S.* blares out.

Flick tosses her ebony locks, rolls her eyes and jerks her head towards the bar. We finally reach it after pushing our way through the hoard for several minutes, ordering G&T's. I glance over to the other girls—Stella has her arm draped around one of the guys in the nearby group and Tiff is throwing her head back—laughing, I think—with another. Anna is MIA. I can't be bothered with any of it and gulp down my drink.

We move to the edge of the dancefloor to a less crowded spot. Flick jigs in time to the music but makes no attempt to move onto the dancefloor. I glance around at the writhing bodies, a mating ritual on full display. It provides a good opportunity to suss out the body language, to understand some of what I've been learning at uni.

My eyes fall on a couple of guys a few metres from us, both periodically turning and looking my way.

'I think they're interested,' Flick yells in my ear.

'Don't' care,' I shout back, but can't help squinting to get a better look, my disdain turning to horror as I realise, I know them—friends of Jakes. Friends who were around when Jake was nosediving but did nothing to stop it. Friends that never even came to his funeral.

Anger bubbles in my veins and before reason sets in, I march over to them, their eyes widening as I approach.

'Call yourself fucking friends!' I lunge towards them, fists clenched at my sides.

'Look ... wait,' one of them mouths back. 'I'm sorry about—'

'Sorry? You're sorry that your so-called friend died of a drug overdose and you left him?' I step back, nostrils flaring. 'Where were you?'

The other steps forward, his shoulders hunched, palms facing upwards. 'He didn't want to know us,' he says.

'Did you even try? Did you even try to save him?'

A look of confusion washes over his face. 'I wasn't even there! How could I have saved him?'

I lunge again, this time fists poised to pound.

'Stop!' he shouts as my hands bash against his chest. 'You fuckin' psycho!'

Flick tries to pull me back as I scream, 'You let him die! It's your fault.'

As I reign blow-upon-blow on him, a hand reaches over and yanks me, and I stumble backwards.

'That's enough!' a booming voice yells.

I turn and come face-to-face with a tall man covered in tatts and wearing dark clothes.

'You need to leave,' he says, clutching my arm and dragging me away.

Flick yells at him to leave me alone, but he ignores her, and I quick step to keep up as he pulls me away.

I thrash and scream, expletives bursting out, but it's no use. I am thrust out of a side door and onto the paved streets of Northbridge, the heavy metal door slamming shut behind me.

It takes a few moments to compose myself, to figure out what just happened, and when I do nausea grips and I vomit against the side of the building, purging the anger, the hatred in one swift but sickly moment.

Shame engulfs me as I wipe my mouth on my arm and check my hair. It's all I can do to stand straight, my guts protesting the trauma I've just put them through. I wander over to the roadside and plonk myself down on the kerb, drawing my knees up to my chin, making myself as small and inconspicuous as I can. Christ knows how long I sit there before a familiar voice calls over.

'Thank god!' Flick yells and sits down next to me, her arm curling around my shoulder. 'You okay?' she says, stroking my hair.

'Think so.'

'What happened in there?'

'Dunno. Just lost it when I saw them—school friends of Jake's.'

'Oh. Sorry hun.'

We remain silent for a while, immersed in our own thoughts. We must look a sight, but then again, we're in Northbridge—this kind of stuff happens every weekend.

'Wanna go home?' Flick asks, pulling her arm away and easing herself up.

I nod. *I want to go home and forget Jake ever existed.*

November 2010

So this is the path I'm taking. The desire to figure out Jake's demise is too important to let go of.

My mum and dad seem so proud as I step up to the stage and collect my graduation certificate. I'm not sure if they were ever signed up to the idea of me being some kind of writer. Perhaps they felt it was nothing more than a hobby, something Jake and I shared that stopped us succumbing to boredom. Perhaps.

Every now and again I pick up a pen and try and put words to paper, try to come up with a story line only, a few sentences in and my mind spins with errant thoughts, my pen no longer moving. Every idea, every plot parked for another day, except that day never comes.

This path is safe. It offers the promise of answers to questions still trolling my mind. This path is the one I must travel in order to keep my sanity and life ticking over. Jake was just too important to me to let go of.

~~~

Flick hugs me after the ceremony, telling me how thrilled she is for me to have reached this far. But what happens now? Where do I go from here? I don't feel ready to start working in this field and want to linger in academia for a while longer—no ties, no long-term plans, no need to be a grown-up just yet.

I've already looked at doing a postgraduate Masters, set my sights on remaining in study for at least another two years.

'We off to the pub to celebrate?' Flick says, linking my arm.

I glance over at my parents.

'You go, darling, we need to get home and sort the cat out.' *Lame excuse.*

'No worries,' I reply, not even caring to challenge them.

Flick and I meet up with the other girls and some uni friends in a small bar in Joondalup. I'm still wearing smart pants and blouse—too formal for the scruffy pub we're in, but I just don't care. The wine is flowing, celebrations are rife and I'm enjoying being the centre of attention ... just this once.

As the afternoon turns to evening and the friends thin out, Flick, me and the girls remain, hitting the wine hard, distancing ourselves from our day-to-day issues. I love times like these and don't want them to end.

We all live in and around Doubleview, so catch the bus home together. I am half-cut, as are the others, a regular occurrence with us girls now. It doesn't bother me. I figure it's all part of twenty-something life, especially when you're a student. No, it doesn't bother me when I'm pissed. It's only afterwards when the shame seeps in and I realise I am in danger of treading the same path Jake did. But who gives a shit right now? We look after each other, look out for each other. *I'm in control, aren't I?*

~~~~

I sit across from the course tutor at Curtin University. She's a strange-looking woman: her hair is dyed brown, but with streaks of grey that almost look deliberate. Her eyes sparkle, but her cheeks are sallow, and her skin is pale. I struggle to warm to her, even though she is nothing but friendly.

'Your results from your degree are very good,' she says.

'Thanks,' I reply, not knowing what else to say.

'There will be a heavy practical load on this course. Do you feel ready for that?'

'I think so.' I try to sound confident—sitting tall in my seat and keeping my tone even. 'I feel it's the natural next step for me.'

She nods. 'We'd be pleased to have you on board. You'll need to fill out the registration asap and send it through.'

'I will.'

'Welcome to the course, Miss Reid.' She gets up and thrusts her hand towards me.

I reach over and shake it—it reminds me of a wet fish—then say my goodbyes and leave. And just like that, the next two years of my life are organised; an MA. Two years of in-depth study, practical assignments and work experience. Two years of cementing what I've learned so far. Two years until the answers click into place ... I hope.

February 2011

Curtin campus is huge and so different from what I've been used to, like I was in a playful kindy and am now starting primary school. Although the summer has been long and hot—and this day is no different—a shiver runs through me and nausea lingers. What have I let myself in for?

My quest strengthened somewhere between finishing high school and graduating, a five-year plan emerging. I will become a Clinical Psychologist. I want to know what happens to people when addiction takes hold. I *need* to know it all only, there are so many things that fill me with dread, take me far outside my comfort zone … like helping others. I have to have practical placements, supervision, apply knowledge in a variety of settings and to a wide and diverse community. It's all so far removed from my earlier dreams of sitting at a desk, tapping away at a keyboard to bring stories to life. But life is like that, isn't it? One minute, an idea takes shape, promises fruition and fulfillment but quickly dissipates when a dose of harsh reality is dealt.

I make my way to my first lecture, knots twisting in my stomach, dread lurking like a monster from the deep, and find a seat in the theatre-like room filled with twenty-somethings, pens and paper laid out in from of them.

A man, scruffy looking with unkempt greying hair, beard and glasses approaches a lectern and coughs. En-masse, eyes dart forward, pens poised. 'Good morning. I'm Carl Friend and contrary to my name, I will NOT be your friend if you don't study hard.' A wry smile crosses his face and titters resound.

Instantly, the tension in the room seems to dissipate like dissolving mist and a guy in the seat next to me leans across and whispers, 'I wonder if that's a psych trick to lull us into a false sense of security?'

I shift round to look at him, smiling. 'Maybe …'

'Connor,' he replies, awkwardly holding out his hand.

'Clara,' I reply, returning the gesture. 'Nice to meet you.'

The lecture seems to whizz by, and I spend most of it scribbling notes against the handouts we've been given and flicking through pages of the accompanying textbooks. By the end of the two hours, my head is buzzing and I'm busting for a wee.

As I make my way out from the row I've been seated on, Connor rushes over. 'Hey Clara—wait up.'

He catches up to me. 'Are you free for a coffee?'

'Sure, but I need to use the bathroom first.' Thankfully, lecture time is far less than in my previous course and there is ample time to study, research, and socialise.

After the pit stop, I meet Connor in the café near the main library and we sit outside after ordering our drinks.

'What do you think of it so far?' he asks.

'Yeah … it seems good. You?'

'Dunno yet. Seems like a huge step-up from my previous course.'

'What did you study?' I notice dyed blond curls cupping his face and neck, brown eyes and honey-mocha skin. He's an attractive guy, but something tells me he's not my type.

'Counselling here,' he says, wiping imaginary crumbs from his mouth.

'You?'

'Psychology at ECU.'

'That's why I haven't seen you before. Where're you from?'

'Doubleview. Well, at the moment. Live with my folks.'

'Me too. Although I'm moving out in a few weeks— my girlfriend's working so we're renting a place together.'

'Nice. How long have you been together?'

'Since 7th year.'

'Wow! That's a lasting love-story.'

He grins, his eyes sparkling, and somehow in that moment I know we will be good friends even though something in the dark recesses of my brain is pondering the idea of a love that prevails, where loss is not a factor in everyday life and emotions.

~~~

Connor and his girlfriend, Deanna, have finally moved in together and are having a house-warming party, and because Connor and I have become firm friends, I'm invited and am bringing the girls along too, except Tiff who's loved up with her latest beau for the night.

When we arrive at Connor's unit in Ellenbrook, music is already blaring from inside and we can hear raised voices—the party has already started, but thanks to some cheap wine, the girls and I are already tanked-up and raring to go.

We enter through a mesh flyscreen and make our way to the source—a lounge room filled with young and old already swaying in time to a thumping beat. It takes a tour of the room and outside to locate Connor, who's deep in conversation with a couple of guys. I tap him on the shoulder, and he spins to face me.

'You made it!' he shouts above the din and flings his arms around me.

'Hey ... great party,' I reply, stepping back.

'Thanks. Let me introduce you to—' but before he finishes, one of the guys interrupts, pushing himself between us.

'Dan,' he says, holding out his hand.

'Clara,' I shout, returning the gesture and noticing Dan's floppy brown hair and bulging guns.

Flick jabs me in the ribs and I flush from head to toe.

~~~~~

It's official—Dan and I are dating. After a few false starts, due in part to his work and my erratic timetable, we have successfully navigated through two coffee dates in the city, one hot and spicy dinner at Long Chim's, and a trip to the cinema to see 'Black Swan'— not exactly a romantic flick.

Dan has blown me away with his infectious passion for life, his obsession with mountain biking and all things fitness related, and a sense of humour verging on black. He's also very easy on the eye and I can't help checking out the defined curves of his athletic body at every opportunity. Even though we are chalk and cheese with many things, our glue is the love of stories; books and movies produce endless hours of deep discussion—so much like the good old days with Jake.

But even though we have pages that are the same and seem to share a mutual attraction, I am taking things slow. Dan is the first guy in a long while to tick boxes and pass the mental tests I throw out. So far, there is no 'ick' factor. Things look promising.

～～～

Exercise does not feature on any of my pages so when Dan suggests an early morning jog along Scarborough Beach, I am winded on two counts: firstly, I've avoided that beach since Jake was found there and have no desire to visit it now, and secondly, my fitness is probably somewhere in the 40th percentile. This does not bode well for our blossoming relationship as it means big reveals could happen that may dissolve some of the glue.

A knock on the door signals Dan's early morning arrival only, I'm not dressed in jogging pants and runners and instead open the door with sleep still in my eyes and a steaming mug of Moccona in hand.

'Morning Clara!' Dan's says beaming. 'Oh. You're not ready yet.'

'Yeah ... about that,' I reply sheepishly. 'Come in. I have something to tell you.'

He follows me into the lounge room and sits on the sofa. 'You okay?'

'I'm good.' Still standing, I shuffle from one foot to the other. 'Um ... do you want a coffee?'

He frowns, brown eyes dimmed. 'What's this about, C?'

Placing my mug on the side table, I plop down in the chair opposite mentally preparing what I'm going to say. 'It's nothing, really. It's just that ... well, I know you like your fitness stuff, but it's not really my thing.'

'Guessed as much,' he says grinning and nodding. 'So we're not jogging, then?' He seems hopeful.

'No, I mean ... yes, we can still go for a jog, but you'll have to go easy on me.'

'Of course. No problem. But?'

'But there is something I need to tell you about—'

His face hardens. 'Should I be worried?'

'No, it's just that it's something quite personal and I haven't been comfortable enough in past relationships to talk about it.'

He leans forward, interest piqued.

'Just before I turned sixteen, Jake, my brother, died.' I take deep breaths to steady myself as the memories flood back.

Dan rises, moving over to the arm of the chair and parking himself on it as his hand lightly touches my shoulder. 'I'm so sorry,' he breathes.

'It's okay,' I say looking up into furrowed eyes. 'He was found on Scarborough Beach, in the wash. An overdose.'

'Christ,' Dan says scooping me into his arms. 'I didn't realise—'

'You couldn't know. It's not something I talk about.'

He pulls back, cupping my face in his warm hands and plants a soft kiss on my lips. 'Thanks for telling me, C. Wish I could've been there for you.'

'That's sweet, Dan. Thank you,' I reply, turning my face away so he can't see the tears pooling.

'Hey ... you know you can talk to me about anything.' His fingers brush the side of my cheek. 'I want you to feel safe with me.'

Turning back to look at him, I smile and reply, 'I want that too.'

We don't make it out for that jog. Instead, Dan and take the next step in turning our glue into cement.

November 2011

Dan places the spare door key to his three by two rental unit in Duncraig into my hands, his smile broader than the Swan River. I can't believe this is really happening and am shocked with how effortless it has been reaching this point.

'Welcome home,' he beams, planting a kiss on my lips.

I've stayed at his place so many times it already feels homely, but with boxes filled with clothes, books and knick-knacks placed in every room, I am glowing from the inside with the realisation that both Dan and I have willingly taken the next step towards permanency.

'I'll go and help Connor unpack the trailer and bring the rest of your stuff in,' he says, then winks. 'Put the kettle on.'

Grinning from ear-to-ear, I head into the kitchen and fill up the kettle, already knowing where most things are.

We have given ourselves the rest of the day to get everything unpacked and in place before my parents, Flick, Anna, Connor and Deanna come over for an intimate house-warming dinner, aka takeout pizza and SSB.

After making the boys a much-needed cuppa and busying myself with opening boxes like it's Christmas, the day drifts steadily along until Dan and I are eventually alone and cosied up on the new couch we bought together with a bottle of wine, chips and hummus.

My first night in my new home—our home. It seems surreal, and yet I am revelling in what feels like the beginning of my new life, one filled with love, comfort, and most of all, safety.

'Thanks for all of this,' I say to Dan, gazing into eyes that pull me in like a magnet.

'Thanks for agreeing to move in,' he replies, face glowing. 'Love you, C.'

'Love you too,' I reply, snuggling up to my man.

~~~

You know someone really loves you when they sacrifice something important to them for your comfort and wellbeing. Dan has cleared out his gym equipment from one of the spare rooms to make way for a new desk so I can have my own workspace.

The window in my new office looks out onto the small patch of garden behind the house. Dan is not a keen gardener, so over a few weekends I convince him to cut the grass and tidy up the flower bed to make it more of an inspirational view for days when I'm struggling to get through the reams of work still to be done on my Masters, especially as I'm nearing the end of the first year and shitloads of assignments are due in. He has gone over and above to accommodate me, which is amazing considering that it was his place to start with and he still foots the majority of the rent and bills as my part-time 'checkout chick' job doesn't pay much. Yes, Dan has sacrificed so much already to be with me. He's a damn good catch.

~~~~~

Another of Dan's passions is footy, and every other weekend he and some of his mates gather at one of their pads for a footy and beer evening watching live games or reruns from when the West Coast Eagles were in fine form.

AFL bores me rigid, so when 'footy nights' are at our place, I usually make myself scarce by having a catch-up with the girls, mostly nights out in Northbridge. It's a chance for us to regroup, gossip and plan out the next phases of our lives, although Flick remains staunchly single as her job as a fledgling real estate agent keeps her busy, Tiff is between boyfriends, Stella's gone long-term with her partner, and Anna, rising through the ranks in the marketing department of City of Perth, is in a steady relationship with Mia, a girl she met at uni.

So when we meet up in The Moon for drinks and a nibble, it's no wonder we have oodles to talk about, each taking our turn in giving the lowdown on our lives before the conversations turn to the deeper, more profound aspects such as 'how good is Dan in bed?' and 'when did you last have a PAP smear?' These are the things that make us tick, that bind us together for what I hope will be lifelong journeys. These girls are my family, Flick especially, and even when there are blackout phases or embargoes on the harder aspects of our individual lives—such as when Jake died, or when Tiff broke up with her last beau who she thought was the love of her life—we always come back together and are always there for each other. Safety nets.

'How's the honeymoon?' Tiff asks brashly.

I roll my eyes, knowing she's taking the piss. 'It's really great,' I reply, shooting her a big, fake smile. 'How's the dry season?'

'Below the belt, Straight-jacket!' Anna yells, chortling as Tiff jabs me in the side almost tipping my wine.

Laughter erupts around our little table as we continue our merriment, enjoying the precious few hours we have free.

And this is how we roll. God, I love these girls! Just as well Dan likes them too because this passion is one I wouldn't ever want to sacrifice.

December 2011

The reverse-cycle aircon in the house has packed up just in time for Perth's first forty-degree day of the season. Dan and I are both in shitty moods. He's been on the phone several times to the real estate agents to try and get it fixed, but the landlord is on holiday and they can't reach him to get the go-ahead for the repairs to be done. Thankfully, Dan's mates have rallied around and supplied several fans, which are making life just about bearable as we wait for the damn air con to be fixed.

Dan is staying late at his personal training work at Doherty's Gym, making the most of more comfortable surrounds even though it's filled with sweaty clients. I, on the other hand, am flitting between lectures, part-time work and sitting in my stuffy little office with nothing but a desk fan for company. Tensions are flaring.

After eight days of sweltering, respite finally arrives when a workman turns up at the crack of dawn with a toolbox and a smile to fix the faulty unit. I am so elated that I throw my arms around him when he's done, telling him he's saved my life only, I'm not joking. But the relief is short-lived.

'What's for dinner?' Dan asks after arriving home, kissing my cheek and dropping his gym bag on the sofa.

'Takeout?' I shrug.

'Too busy to cook again, were you?' he replies sarcastically.

'I've been working too, you know!'

'Yeah ... I can see that.' He gestures to the books and files stashed haphazardly on the dining table. 'What's wrong with your office?'

'It was too hot in there to work,' I snap back. 'Besides, there's nothing stopping you from making dinner.'

'I've been at work all fucking day!' His jaw clenches as he barks his retort.

'So have I!' I yell, clenching my fists. 'I know I'm not doing actual work like you, but this is just as important.'

'It's not paying the bills, though, is it?' His face hardens and he tuts loudly.

'I'm doing my best, Dan. It's not my fault my pay is shit, is it?' Anger bubbles as I plead my case. 'What the fuck is this about?'

Dan sighs, his face softening. 'Nothing ...'

'It's clearly not nothing. Tell me.'

'The rent's going up by $50 a fortnight.' He runs his hand through his hair. 'I wanted to surprise you with a trip to Bali for Christmas, but I don't think I can afford it now.'

'Oh Dan ... I'm so sorry,' I whisper as guilt consumes me. 'I don't need a holiday to know that you love me.' I cast him a feeble smile.

He shakes his head. 'We both could do with a break, but—'

I grab hold of him and hug him tightly, hoping to reassure him that all will be okay in the only way I can. 'Dan—I can get another job, tighten our belts until I graduate and get a proper job. It'll be okay ... you'll see.'

~~~

With Christmas looming and university finished for the year, I take the opportunity to do some last-minute shopping with Tiffany. Most of it is window shopping, given my less-than-desirable financial status, but I manage to find some inexpensive gifts for my nearest and dearest: a floaty scarf for Mum, a Dremel attachment for Dad, a secret Santa gift to exchange with the girls, and a pair of compression shorts I found on sale for Dan. As I make these meagre purchases, I keep telling myself that it's the thought that counts, even though Dan's gesture of a holiday in Bali surely trumps it all. I also try to reassure myself that this is only a temporary thing; as soon as I graduate, I'll get a well-paid job in Clinical Psychology and be more than able to contribute to the pot. But these thoughts hang heavy, building on the pressure to get my shit together.

~~~

No-one mentions how stressful Christmas can be when you're in a relationship, and not just because of the need to please and pamper, but also having to accommodate the expectations of family. It's no surprise then, that Dan and I are having to navigate our way around both our families' invitations for dinner without upsetting each party, leaving very little time for us to enjoy our first Christmas together alone.

Dan's huge family are second-generation Pinelli's with a stone fruit business in the hills of Kalamunda. Christmas dinner consists of each family bringing a plate to a combined celebration at a nominated family's home. How the hell they all manage to cater for upwards of fifty people each year is beyond me and makes my family gatherings seem intimate. This year, Dan's Aunt in Pinjarra is playing host, meaning we have to drive for a couple of hours south of Perth to the middle of nowhere and be there by midday, bringing a savoury plate and two Secret Santa gifts. This is so outside of my comfort zone and has caused friction with my family who expected me to be at home from dusk til dawn. After we finish at the Pinelli gathering, we then have to drive back to my parents' home, hopefully in time for dinner. This gives me and Dan a scant few hours in the morning to celebrate Christmas together for the first time and hopefully create our own traditions. I'm exhausted already.

When I open my eyes on Christmas morning, Dan is already up and about, quietly banging around in the kitchen. I clamber out of bed, and after a pee stop, head into the kitchen where he's waiting for me with a steaming mug of coffee and pancakes.

'Merry Christmas, beautiful,' he says, his eyes glinting, and he walks around the island bench and wraps me up in strong arms.

'Now this is the kind of Christmas I'd hoped for,' I whisper, nuzzling into his neck.

'I have a little something for you, well—two things to be exact.'

'Dan! I thought we were going to only buy each

other one thing?' I protest while secretly thrilled.

'I know, I know. They're only small gifts, so I hope you like them.' He strides over to our little tinsel tree and pulls out two rectangle-shaped gift-wrapped boxes and hands them over.

My eyes light up and I tear at the wrapping on the smaller box, finally revealing a snap box housing a Pandora bracelet and Christmas tree charm. 'Dan! You shouldn't have. It's gorgeous.' I beam.

'Here, let me put it on for you,' he says, pulling out the bangle and clipping it shut around my wrist. 'I thought I could buy you a charm each year. Make it special, you know?'

'I thought we weren't spending a lot.'

'I saved up for this one,' he says, winking. 'Open the other.'

I pull apart the wrapping, although I already know it's a book judging by the shape and weight. As I rip off the final piece of paper, the title comes into sight, *The Book Thief*, and what was giddy delight morphs into horror and I stare at Dan, mouth agape.

'Don't you like it, C?' Dan says. 'You told me you'd lost the copies you had, so I thought it must be a favourite read.' Dan's face drops, eyebrows arching as he cottons on to my reaction not being what he'd hoped for.

I am lost for words. Can't explain what I'm feeling in that moment, but acutely aware of tears pricking the corners of my eyes. 'It's fine,' I say, and flee to the safety of the bathroom, locking the door behind me.

'Clara?' Dan pleads tapping on the door, 'I'm sorry … I honestly thought you'd like it.'

'Just give me a minute!' I snap, instantly feeling guilty. 'I just need a moment to gather my thoughts.'

I hear Dan sigh, but he says nothing more as I slump down on the loo and try and figure out what's going on in my head, all-the-while memories of Jake flitting in and out.

When I finally come out, Dan is sitting on the sofa twiddling a Lego Masters kit bought for him by one of his mates. He looks up as I slope into the lounge room.

'You okay, C?' His face is pale, and he doesn't look me in the eye.

'Yeah … look, Dan—I'm sorry about that. It brought back memories, that's all.'

'I'm so sorry. If I'd known—'

'You didn't know, and it's okay. I love it. Really.' I'm not even convincing myself but resolve to pull up from this nose-dive. 'Hey, how about you open your present.'

He smiles, one that doesn't reach his eyes, then dives under the tree, grabs the remaining gift and shreds at the wrapping. 'Compression shorts. Awesome! Thanks, C.' And he genuinely looks delighted.

By the time Christmas Day wraps up and Dan and I have finally returned home, we are both so exhausted and bloated that the only thing we want to do is sleep. This doesn't bode well for future traditions. Surely lovemaking is a must on Christmas Day?

March 2012

'Clara Reid,' the prison warden bellows, heaving open a thick metal door leading to a tiny office.

A man sitting behind a grey melamine desk looks up at me, glasses tilted on his nose.

'Welcome Clara. Please—have a seat,' he says smiling.

I sit opposite. 'Thanks. Nice to meet you Mr Cox,' I reply as butterflies jostle for position in my stomach.

'Anthony. Call me Anthony,' he says, offering his hand.

I shake it, hoping he can't feel mine trembling.

'So, Clara, how are you feeling about your placement?'

'A bit nervous,' I admit, 'but I'm looking forward to it.'

'You've been highly recommended by your university supervisor. I hope you know what you've let yourself in for.' He tosses me a grin, raising bushy brows. 'We'll start with the two-hour group session. You'll be observing at first, taking notes about the inmates in the program. We'll debrief afterwards.'

'Okay,' I reply, feigning a confident smile.

'We start in half-an-hour, so let's grab a coffee and I'll show you around.'

The butterflies start performing backflips.

~~~~~

Anthony and I sit in the middle of a large room with magnolia walls, grey carpet and plastic chairs circled around us. I glance at the walls adorned with posters about drug and alcohol abuse and tacky motivational quotes like, 'It may seem like a mountain, but we'll help you climb it.'

I balance a notepad on my lap and clasp my pen like it's a lifeline. Anthony tucks in his shirt and pulls a whiteboard marker from his pocket. 'Ready?'

'Uh-huh,' I reply, twisting my fingers, almost dropping the pen.

'Most of them do this to score brownie points to get a shorter sentence,' Anthony whispers, leaning towards me, 'although a few genuinely want to sort themselves out.'

Jake's lifeless face flashes in my mind reminding me of why I'm here only, six years of studying psychology at uni have barely scratched the surface.

I hate the fucking sea.

'Clara—' Anthony whispers, pulling me back. 'They're arriving.'

I straighten and turn to watch figures dressed in navy pants and grey, short-sleeved shirts trundle single-file into the room. Wolf-whistles ring out as I eye each man.

'Guys,' Anthony says. 'Manners.'

I can do this.

Mumbles, and a chorus of, 'sorry,' intertwine with scraping chairs. I count eleven men in total, each taking a seat in our circle.

'Alright. Let's start by—' Anthony is interrupted by another man darting into the room. 'Michael—you're late.'

'Sorry Tony,' Michael replies, scurrying to a seat opposite.

Michael looks across at me. 'I'll make sure I'm not in future,' his lips curling around a thick accent I can't place.

Penetrating blue eyes, so much like Jake's, lock me in like a tractor beam and the hairs on my arms stand tall.

'Okay guys ... this is Clara,' Anthony announces, pulling me away from Michael's hold. 'She'll be helping me for the next six weeks, so be nice. Right, who wants to go first?'

A youthful-looking Aboriginal man puts his hand up. 'I'll go, Anthony.'

'How are you doing today, Adam?'

'Ah man ... I'm tired, y'know. Fitzy kept me awake all night with his farting!'

Laughter erupts around the room.

'That's enough.' Anthony frowns. 'Adam, start again please.'

'Yeah ... sorry,' he sniggers. 'I'm feeling good. Gonna do some community service today.'

'And what are you looking forward to the most?'

'Decent food,' he replies, beaming a toothy grin.

Several of the men jeer and clap.

Anthony shakes his head and grins. 'Okay. Who's next?'

One-by-one the men share how they are and what they are looking forward to. I jot down each one's name, and features such as curly black hair and tribal tattoo as an aide memoir.

'I'm looking forward to this,' Michael says when it's his turn.

'Oh?' Anthony says.

'Well ... I haven't seen a decent bit of skirt for nearly eighteen months.'

I shrivel in my seat as Michael and the others regale in his comment.

Anthony shakes his head and tuts.

'Sorry Clara ...' Michael says, locking eyes with me for the briefest of moments before looking away.

~~~

'How do you feel the session went today, Clara?' Anthony asks me across the desk in his office.

'Okay, I think,' I reply, writing down some final notes.

'They push the boundaries, but you can pull them

up and they will toe the line. They're not a bad bunch.'

'I was expecting worse, to be honest.'

'This lot are not hard-core criminals, just made some bad choices. And don't worry about Michael—he likes to act-out.'

'What's his story?' I ask, feigning indifference, hoping Anthony hasn't noticed my piqued interest.

'Strange, really. From a well-off family.' He rubs his chin. 'Went to university and had a promising life but was charged with drunk and disorderly offences before he finished. His parents pushed for this rehab program.'

'Really?' I reply frowning.

'Guess they'd had enough. Couldn't get him off the grog, so thought it best to get him banged up and into rehab.'

If only we'd done that with Jake.

~~~~~

'How'd your first day of prac go?' Dan asks as he chops onions and carrots for a spag bol.

'Good, I think. Not what I expected,' I reply munching on a stick of celery in between glugs of wine.

'How so?'

'Dunno really. Guess I thought they'd be a bunch of rough-nuts, but they don't seem too bad.'

'They'd hardly let you loose on a bunch of murderers now, would they!' Dan scoffs. 'Think you'll like it there?'

Michael's face pops unsolicited into my mind. 'I think so,' and I shake my head to free the image. 'When's dinner going to be ready?'

'Thirty minutes.'

'Great. I've got my journal to fill in so give me a shout when it's ready, okay?'

Dan turns and tosses me a smile and I grab the wine and head off to my office.

I sit idly in front of the laptop screen trying to piece together the main topics and themes of the day's session for my uni journal, but all I can hear in my head is Michael's voice saying 'sorry' and imagine his ocean-blue eyes boring into me.

Shit!

Dan's booming voice carries into the office. 'C! Dinner!'

I gaze at the screen quickly re-reading the scant paragraphs of notes I've managed to type and sigh. 'Coming,' I reply, snapping the laptop shut.

April 2012

'What are you writing?' Michael leans over my seat from behind, his warm breath brushing the back of my neck.

Startled, I try to flip over the notepad in my lap and it drops to the floor. 'Nothing,' I reply. 'Work stuff.' I scramble to pick it up almost butting heads with Michael as he reaches down to get it.

Our fingers lightly brush as he hands it back, his eyes staring into mine.

I grab the pad and look up at the clock. 'You're early—' I stammer, the room constricting around me.

'I write, y'know,' he says, crouching in front of me.

'Really? Like what?'

'Dunno … stuff. Life, y'know.'

'Written anything recently?' I tuck a stray strand of hair behind my ear.

'Started my life story, but I guess it's still a work-in-progress,' he chuckles.

'I can relate.' I lower my gaze, praying he can't see the heat rising in my cheeks.

'What're you working on?'

'Nothing much,' I sigh. 'Can't seem to get the right

words out.'

'I'd like to read your work sometime,' Michael says, his eyes pulling me in as if I'm diving into an azure sea. I don't even notice the other men filing into the room until Michael scurries away and Anthony plops down beside me.

'Right, gentlemen, good to see you all,' he says. 'Clara—you want to check in first.'

'Oh ... um, okay,' I reply, thrown-off by his invitation. 'Well ... I guess I'm okay and looking forward to hearing from you all.'

'Anything you'd like to say about our last session?' Anthony asks me, putting me on the spot.

I glance around the room, trying to think of something smart and useful to say, but Michael's cheeky grin captures my gaze and heat rises in my face. 'Um ... no, don't think so.' I squeak, wishing a sink hole would appear and swallow me.

'Okay then,' Anthony says, 'Let's go around and check-in. Michael—you first, seen as you're here on time.'

'Thanks, Tony,' Michael replies, his tone cocky. 'I am really good and looking forward to today's session.'

'Anything you want to bring up?'

'Not yet,' he says, shooting me a wicked grin sending my pulse soaring.

Anthony works his way around the group until the last man has checked in. 'So today we'll be talking about boundaries, about what are healthy boundaries and what are not.' He shoots a glare at Michael and I fidget in my seat as a nervous cough escapes me.

~~~

'Don't let him get under your skin,' Anthony says as we walk through the dark corridor towards his office, steaming mugs of coffee in hand. 'He's harmless but will try and push your buttons.'

Is that all he's doing?

'It's fine, Anthony. Honestly.' I'm not sure who I'm trying to convince.

'Well, just let me know if he gets too much.'

'I will, thanks,' I reply, inwardly chastising myself because I already know he's dug the hole and is climbing in.

Anthony lets out a sneeze that sounds like a dog barking and pulls out a hanky from his pocket and blows hard. 'Damn it!' he says. 'Think I'm getting a cold.'

May 2012

'Ode to Joy' rings out from my mobile and I scramble around the sofa trying to find it, finally pulling it out from between two cushions.

'Hello. This is Clara.'

Several coughs resound, then a croaky voice says, 'Clara, it's Anthony.'

'Hi Anthony. How you going?'

'Not good. Listen, I have a cold and can't come into work today. I can ring the prison and cancel the session, or if you feel able, you can take it and I'll arrange for one of the wardens to be on hand. What do you reckon?'

Panic wrenches as I imagine an unruly bunch of men running rings around me as I try and guide them through the session.

'Clara? You there?' Anthony splutters.

'Yep, err … yes. Still here. Just thinking.'

'You don't have to do the session. I can cancel.'

Mind spinning, I ponder the idea further as Dan walks into the open-plan living area and tosses me a grin. Taking a deep breath, I reply, 'no, it's okay. I can do it.'

'Great,' Anthony says. 'I was going to talk about

coping mechanisms during moments of temptation. Are you happy to cover it?'

'Yes. I think so.'

'There's some notes in my drawer for the session. Use those to guide you through the topic and exercises. Okay?'

'Okay,' I reply, a mental picture of Anthony's desk forming. 'Shall I call the prison and let them know for you? You sound really bad.'

'Gee thanks,' he says, and on cue starts coughing again. 'No, I'll do it. Needs to come from me.'

'No worries.'

'Give me a call if you're struggling, or let the warden know, and we'll debrief before the next session. Sure you're okay to do this?'

'I'm sure,' I reply, although not entirely convinced myself.

'Good luck, and I'll see you soon.'

'See you soon, Anthony. And I hope you feel better soon.' I end the call and stand stock-still as my mind races.

Dan strides over. 'Who was that?' he says.

'Anthony. He's got man-flu and needs me to run today's session.'

'You up for that?'

'I bloody hope so.'

~~~

My gut twists as I set up the room, adopting Anthony's seat like a throne as the men walk in.

Michael's voice emanates above the mumblings. 'Where's Tony?'

'He's sick, so I'm running the group today.' The temperature in the room seems to skyrocket and sniggers circle.

'Doesn't mean you can all take the piss.' I boom, trying to sound authoritative.

'Yes miss,' come the chants, and I shrivel like a withering leaf.

I clear my throat, straighten my back and glance over at the warden for peace of mind. 'Let's check in. I'll start—I'm feeling confident that we'll have a productive session.'

Michael fixes his gaze on me, but I can't hold it, afraid he'll see how he's unhinging me.

He's the first to check in. 'I'm not sure how I feel today, Clara.'

'Oh?' I frown.

'You intimidate me.'

What?

'You feel I'm intimidating?' A shiver meanders down my back as snorts dance around the room.

'Yeah. Like ... if I say something wrong you might report me.' I swear his eyes are glinting.

'This is a safe space, Michael,' I reply, trying my best to take control.

'You did ask—'

'Do you have anything else to say?' I say, snapping.

He tosses me a wink.

Breathe, Clara. Just breathe.

'Right,' I say, trying to channel my inner Anthony, 'Adam—you're next,' and shoot a scowl at Michael.

~~~

The rest of the session passes more smoothly, Michael's behaviour tempered, and our discussions around coping mechanisms seem to have been reasonably well-received.

I start packing away chairs as the men file out of the room, but as I turn to grab the last one, Michael blocks my way.

'Did you need something, Michael?' I eye him scornfully.

He inches closer, putting a hand in his pocket. 'Here.' He pulls out a folded piece of paper and thrusts it towards me.

'What is it?' I grab the paper and step back as confusion and a flush of heat volley for attention.

He cocks an eyebrow and walks away.

'Michael?'

I glance around to see if anyone saw this clandestine moment, my fingers trembling, my heart rate zooming as I unfold the paper and read the note:

Clara,

Sorry for being a pain.

Michael.

That's it?

~~~~

'I need to tell you about Michael and show you this—' I hand the note to a still-snuffling Anthony and recount Michael's comments during the previous session.

'Always pushing the boundaries,' Anthony replies, tutting. 'He's a funny one, though. Doesn't like to be thought badly of. Apologises whenever he gets the chance.'

'Do you think I should say something to him?'

'Ordinarily, yes—but he was released on Monday.'

My heart cracks, just a little …

October 2012

The girls and Dan rally around me as I clasp my certificate and straighten my graduation cap.

'You did it!' Flick squeals. 'Congratulations.'

'Yeah … congrats, Straight-jacket!' Anna says laughing. 'God help all those poor souls needing *your* help.'

'Very funny,' I reply, mock scowling, but inside I'm swelling with pride.

Dan wraps an arm around my waist and kisses my cheek. 'Proud of you, C.'

'Get a room, you two!' Tiff says, pretending to vomit. 'There's plenty of time for that when you get home. Time to party!'

'And that's my cue to leave you girls to it before it gets too messy,' Dan says, unfurling his arm and pulling his car keys from his trouser pocket. 'See you later and be good.' His lips brush mine and he heads off out of the uni hall.

'Girls, I do believe it's wine o'clock,' I say, putting my arms on Flick and Anna's shoulders. 'Let's get out of here!'

After spending several hours in the uni bar, the four of us wait outside in the warm evening sunshine waiting for a taxi to take us into the city. Already pissed, and having changed into more appropriate night-out attire aka red mini dress and too-high heels, I cling on to my girls as we loudly chatter about life, love and everything in between until the taxi pulls up and we clamber in.

I love nights out like these, not only because I can escape the realities of life for a short period of time, but also because these girls are my tribe, the ones who know me best, warts and all. I wouldn't have made it through some of the highs and lows of my life without them and I know they will support me no matter what, as I will them.

As more wine is drunk, the conversation shifts to our partners, specifically Dan.

'How's life in the love shack?' Tiff asks, always the one to jump in at the deep end.

'Good. Why do you ask?'

'No reason,' she replies, sipping wine through a straw. 'Just saw how loved-up you two still are. Was it just for show?'

'What do you mean?'

'Well … Flick said you and Dan had been arguing a lot lately.'

'Did she now.' I turn and glare at Flick who just shrugs. 'What else did she say?'

'That was it mostly. Just that you'd had quite a few ding-dongs since moving in together.'

'I never said that,' Flick says, snarling at Tiff. 'I said that you'd had a FEW spats over silly stuff ... normal stuff.'

'Yeah ... like you've never had blow-outs with your partners over silly shit,' I spit. 'Oh wait ... you've never been with someone long enough for it to get to that stage.'

'Fuck off, C. That's below the belt.'

'Ladies, ladies,' Anna says, hands up. 'No need to turn on each other. We're here to celebrate, remember?'

Tiff rolls her eyes. 'Sorry, C,' and takes another slurp.

'Me too,' I reply sheepishly. 'But for the record, me and Dan are fine.'

~~~

'Welcome Miss Reid, please take a seat.'

I park myself in a chair opposite the two people interviewing me and smooth down my skirt.

'I'm Hadley Norman, Senior Psychologist at the school, and this is my colleague Jane Wilson—Vice Principal.'

'Hello,' I say, reaching forward and shaking their hands.

'So you're applying for the School Counsellor position. What is it that interests you in the role?' Hadley continues.

'Um ... well, I am wanting to help kids who may be struggling with their day-to-day realities, especially where there may be substance abuse in families.'

Hadley nods and flicks through papers on her desk. 'I see you majored in Alcohol and Addiction Studies. What led you to those?'

I pause, Jake's face appearing centre stage in my mind. 'My brother died of an overdose when I was younger. I guess it made me want to understand what happened to him.' I feel flustered as I recount my motives and notice that both women are jotting down notes, the desire strong to know what they're writing.

'Was it just a need to understand, or something more?'

'Oh ... yes, I wanted to understand so that I could help other people afflicted or affected by substance abuse. I saw a counsellor after my brother died, and that helped me a lot.'

They both continue making notes, rattling my composure.

'Your resume says that you've had Practicums in a Low Security Prison for men and an Aged Care Facility. How do you think those experiences could be used in a High School Setting?'

I stare across at the two women like a rabbit caught in headlights, racking my brains for a suitable response, but the answer is I don't see how they translate because the reality is, I'm not even sure I want to do this.

～～～

'How'd the interview go?' Dan asks as I drop my keys on the kitchen bench and sit down at the table.

'Not great,' I reply, sighing, 'and my head's banging.'

'Why, what happened?' He opens a bottle of wine, pours two glasses and passes one over.

Taking a long glug, my shoulders slumping, I reply, 'Just don't think I'm cut out for this.'

'Huh?' his face sours.

'I mean ... working with kids.' *Yeah ... that's what I mean.*

'It's only your first interview. There'll be more, I'm sure,' Dan says, reaching over and squeezing my hand.

I toss him a half-smile and return focus to my wine.

～～～

Dan has gone over to a mate's for footy night, so Flick is at my place helping me polish off another bottle of wine.

'Do you not want to be a Psych, or just not work with kids?' she asks, her legs stretched over mine on the sofa.

'Dunno,' I reply ruefully, staring at a dark speck on the ceiling. 'Kids, probably.'

'You don't sound sure.'

'Maybe I'm not. I can't help but wonder if all this study has actually answered the questions I had about Jake dying, helped me understand it/him more.'

'What does Dan think?'

I huff. 'His only concern is me getting a job so we can go on holiday.'

'I'm sure that's not the case,' Flick says rolling her eyes, always one to see the good in people. 'Have you actually talked to him about it?'

'Sort of ...'

'And what does that mean?'

'Well I can hardly tell him I don't know what I want to do when he's kept me off the streets and helped fund my studies, can I!'

'So you haven't, then,' she says flatly. 'Don't you think you should?'

'No. No, I don't. The guy's sacrificed so much for me that if I pussy-foot around workwise it'll probably be the straw that breaks the camel's back.'

'I thought things were good between you?'

'They are, but ...'

'But what?'

'Well, you know. Relationships can be hard work.'

'And that's why you need to be honest with him otherwise you'll create a wedge that'll get harder to remove.'

I nod in agreement only, there's a lot about me Dan has yet to know ... to understand, things relating to Jake and the impact his death had on me. I'm not sure I can ever let that out ... not even to my nearest and dearest.

August 2014

With a thumping heart and grinning like a Cheshire cat, I sign the bottom of the lease agreement and slide it back across the desk to Janine, owner-caretaker of Blossom Hill Wellness Centre. She scans over it for a few moments, then signs and dates it and walks over to the printer to take a copy.

'That all seems to be in order,' she says extending her hand towards me. 'Congratulations, Miss Reid. I look forward to seeing you soon.'

Shaking her hand and still grinning, I reply, 'Thank you so much. Fingers crossed I get enough clients to make it worthwhile.'

Janine tosses a smile and passes me an envelope containing keys, my deposit receipt and a copy of the lease. And just like that, I am a step closer to running my own Psych practice.

I spend the next few hours assembling my new desk and chair, a small bookshelf and stationary cupboard. Dan brings in some newly purchased armchairs and coffee table (from an Op shop) and positions them in one-half of the room, then sets about putting up a couple of landscape photos in the therapy area along with framed certificates. The final touch is a small brass plaque on the front of the door:

Clara Reid – Clinical Psychologist

I beam as I take it all in—my own space, my practice, a reality made possible by Dan's continued support both emotionally and financially. I only hope it pays off.

~~~~~

Running my own practice comes with many headaches: few clients, mainly sourced through GP referrals, bookkeeping, bill paying, and most-of-all boredom. I spend most of my time Googling random celebrity gossip and playing Candy Crush. This is not how I imagined it being and even Dan is frustrated by my lack of progress.

By the time the financial year ends, and I fill out a tax return, my earnings have amounted to a paltry $3,046.27 and I question whether this journey toward understanding has been worth it.

October 2015

A friend request pops up on my Facebook notifications. A picture of a shamrock appears next to the name 'Michael Moran'. Curiosity bites and I click on the picture.

Scrolling through, I find photos of the Michael. He looks really good: those intense blue eyes still draw me in, and his cheeky smile is infectious.

I shouldn't, should I?

But I can't help myself and click 'Accept'.

With no clients scheduled, I decide to finish work early and head home. And holed up in my cosy home office with a steaming mug of coffee and laptop open and fired up, can't resist the temptation to see if there's been any communication from Michael. Truth be told, my thoughts have drifted to him on more than one occasion wondering what he's been up to, if he still looks as hot as I remember, and what I'd want to say to him if I saw him again.

My pulse zooms as the Messenger box pops up at the bottom of the screen.

'You finished university—that's great.'

I re-read Michael's message over-and-over,

contemplating a reply, settling on, 'Thanks. How are you?'

Within moments a beep rings out as Michael's response comes just as I hear my front door shut.

Dan calls out, 'Clara ... you home?'

'In here.' I snap my laptop shut.

Within seconds he's at my side, arms encircling me. 'Hey,' he says, kissing my cheek.

'Hey back.' I twist round and smile up at him, hiding the niggle deep in my gut. 'How was your day?'

'Better now.' He pecks my forehead and heads off to our bedroom.

My intrigue to see Michael's reply builds like a rumbling volcano, but I need to make dinner, continue as normal.

Damn!

~~~

The following morning after Dan has left for work, I rush to my desk and fire up the laptop, tapping at the keys with fervour and drumming my fingers on the wood as I wait for everything to load. And when Facebook refreshes on my screen, I spot the open message box and butterflies start doing the conga in my gut.

'Not bad,' Michael's message reads. 'I'm working. Driving forklifts. Haven't had a drink since rehab.'

'That's great.' I type back but notice he's offline and my heart sinks.

I sit stock-still front of the laptop suddenly gnawed by parasitic guilt.

~~~

I arrive at work just after 10am and spend a good hour-or-so rifling through the papers strewn across my work desk, filling time. My first client isn't due in until 11:30am, but rather than re-reading my notes to recap on what we've covered, my eyes fall onto a picture of Jake and I fishing together by the Swan River. Even now, eleven years on, the hole he left in my life is cavernous.

'Like two peas in a pod,' my Mum used to say, marvelling at the bond between us.

I adored him—my protector, my confidant, and reminisce of the hours spent poring over books and writing letters and stories. He was always my biggest champion, encouraging me to write more. So why did my letters of love and support matter less than his next fix?

Tears trickle as memories of happier times are bulldozed by the image of his bloated, grey body lying on that cold slab, my parents falling apart as I stand numbed beside them.

~~~

After finishing off with my client and eating a hurriedly concocted salad for lunch, boredom takes hold. I turn to my laptop and indulge in social media to find out what bullshit is happening with so-called 'friends'. As soon as I log in, a message pops up.

'What have you been up to?' Michael writes. 'I see

on your profile you're in a relationship.'

Excitement and a pang of annoyance lock heads as my hands hover over the keyboard, fingers trembling. 'I'm in private practice now,' I type, then hold my breath waiting for his response.

~~~~~

Dan is out for the evening and I have the house to myself for a few hours. And even though rhyme and reason tell me otherwise, I haven't been able to get Michael out of my head. And like an addict, I power up the laptop hoping for my next fix.

'How's business?' comes Michael's message.

'Fine,' I reply, furtive excitement bubbling in my veins.

'How's the partner?'

'None of your business.'

There's a long pause and I worry that I've offended him.

'Sorry,' he finally replies, and I feel bad for my snappy comment.

'No—I'm sorry. Bad day,' I reply, hoping to appease.

'Wanna tell me about it?'

'Just boring. Not sure I'm cut out for listening to peoples' woes.'

'Don't wanna help people?'

'I used to. Anyway, how's yours?'

'Boring 😊'

I chuckle, lightened by his comment. 'Sober for three years—that's great. Sounds like you've turned your life around.'

'Wouldn't say that. Been a hard slog. Still wanna drink, but every day I don't is a blessing.'

'You found God?'

'Nah. People like you save me.'

A pang rises from my gut and I type with fervour, 'The program saved you—I didn't even know you.'

'I want you to know me.'

My fingers freeze over the keys, my heart now racing in fifth gear.

'Clara?'

'Got to go.'

What the hell am I doing?

~~~

Dan wraps his arms around my waist from behind as I apply the finishing touches of makeup.

'You look great,' he says, nuzzling my neck. 'Not sure I want you going out now.'

'Jealous?'

'Always.' He kisses my cheek and leaves the bathroom.

He's a good catch ... isn't he?

I take an Uber into the city and meet up with the girls in a trendy Northbridge bar.

'Watch out, straight-jacket's here!' Tiffany calls as the other three cheer and giggle.

Our sisterhood of five huddles together, moving in unison towards the crowded bar.

'How's practically old-married-couple life?' Tiff mocks.

'Very funny!' I reply. 'Dan's having some mates over to watch the game.'

'Glad you got a pass-out,' Anna shouts above the din unaware I spotted her eyes roll.

We take our drinks and find a spare table, chatting merrily as we catch up. The night progresses quickly with wine and mixers readily consumed. The desire to dance the night away soon beckons so we leave the bar and walk the buzzing Perth streets to the Mint nightclub, passing cafes and bars all still alive with animated conversations and pumping music. Flick links arms with me as the other three lead the way.

'Clara?' A voice carries from across the street. Startled, I turn to see who it is and spot a tall, red-haired man grinning and waving at me—Michael.

I gasp, my pulse zooming from nought to sixty.

He strides across the road towards me, and I can't help noticing how good he looks in dark pants, crisp white shirt, and slicked back hair.

'Shit!' I whisper, bowing my head.

'Who's that?' Flick asks, gawping.

'An old client—'

'You avoiding me, Clara?' Michael calls as he nears.

'No—err ... hi.' I reply, my legs jellifying and threatening to buckle.

Michael eyes us both and smirks. 'You out on the pull?'

'Of course not!' I glare at him. 'I'm out with friends.'

'You look good.'

'I'm Felicity,' Flick thrusts her hand towards Michael, cutting through the spark as I pray for the ground to swallow me up.

'Michael.' He barely grasps her outstretched hand, eyes locked with mine.

'Clara, we need to go.' Flick says, tugging my arm.

'Um ... gotta go. Nice to see you.'

Flick's hold tightens, and she pulls me away.

'You too, Clara. Talk to you on Facebook.'

I turn to look at him, and he nods as I toss him an apologetic smile.

'Wanna tell me who that was?' Flick says marching.

'I told you ... an old client.'

'Uh-huh. And how many "old clients" make you flush like that?' She stops in her tracks and faces me.

'What are you on about?' I feign ignorance.

'I was nearly electrocuted by the charge between you two,' she scoffs. 'Who is he *really*?'

'He was one of the prisoners on my Prac. And I have no idea what you're talking about.' I pull out my arm from her grip and stride away.

~~~

Dan is asleep when I get home.

Still wide awake, I grab a glass of wine from the kitchen and plonk myself down on the sofa.

My mobile chirps. Texts from the girls litter the screen with messages and photos from the night. I swipe through, giggling at our drunken antics, but it doesn't take long for temptation to rear its ugly head. I open Facebook. Michael is online and almost immediately a message pops up and I scan the room just in case.

'Good night?' Michael's message reads.

'Yes,' is all I can think of saying as guilt and glee collide.

'Hope you behaved.'

'That's none of your business.'

'You have a boyfriend. Wouldn't want you to do something stupid.'

But before I can concoct a snappy reply, he follows up with, 'unless it's with me.'

What? 'You can't say that!' I glance around the room again, curling up tighter in a ball on the sofa.

'I just did.'

My head starts to spin as his words register and panic starts to well. 'Go away.'

'Why?'

'I don't want to play games.'

'I didn't ask you to.'

The angel on my shoulder takes a strike. 'Goodbye Michael.' And I'm about to lock my phone when another message pops up.

'Don't go.'

Don't give in, Clara.

But alcohol has made me impetuous and curious. 'What do you want from me?'

I watch three dots wave, then stop, then wave again as he types and re-types. 'Answer me, dammit!' I yell out, then look around, breath held, in case I've woken Dan.

'To know you more.'

I shake my head, thumbs hovering over the phone keys as a gazillion thoughts spiral.

'I can't.' *I mustn't.*

'Why not?'

'I have a partner.'

'Is that really the reason?'

'Yes.'

'Is it serious?'

I fidget from imaginary lumps in the sofa, my breath ragged. 'Of course it is.'

'I'll leave you alone, then.'

Michael's status flips to offline and I stare at the screen, head in hand.

He's just playing with me, just like he always did.

~~~

He's unfriended me from Facebook. Why am I not relieved?

November 2015

As has become customary with my family, we gather around Jake's graveside to commemorate his birthday. Posies of wildflowers placed in metal vases next to the headstone, the headstone itself freshly wiped over. And as has become my own tradition, I place a copy of my last read, Gillian Flynn's 'The Grownup'—an homage to my increasing intrigue with psychological thrillers—in a Ziplock bag and put it by the side of the flowers, retrieving the previous offering now soddened by the elements. I don't know why I keep doing this. Part of me still craves those joyous times spent reading, analysing, discussing all things books with my beloved brother, but why is this not translating into a renewed love of writing?

Tears tumble as we all spend quiet moments reminiscing Jake's life, but they invariably turn to regret for all those moments when we couldn't reach him, when *I* couldn't protect him from himself. And it's times like these that bring the heavy realisation that my efforts, this journey of mine, have amounted to a big fat nothing.

I glance over at my parents, united in their shared grief, leaning on each other for continued support even after all this time.

Do I feel that with Dan?

~~~~~

The girls and I are going out for a Christmas meal at a swanky riverside restaurant. Dan drops me near the Bell Tower, and I walk towards the Lucky Shag bar to meet them.

I'm tottering along on too-high heels and smoothing down my party dress when a voice calls out for spare change from a nearby nook, stopping me in my tracks. A pair of sea-blue eyes stare up at me.

'Michael?' I gasp.

He squints into the still-bright light of early evening. 'Clara?' His face crinkles into a smile. Stale booze wafts on his breath and paled skin peeps from beneath wisps of red stubble.

I spy a bagged bottle clasped in his lap. 'Are you drunk?'

He sits upright. 'Oops.' The bag falls from his lap as he puts a finger to his mouth. 'Shhh. Don't tell anyone.'

I should leave, ignore him like all the other vagrants, but—

I stoop to grab hold of his arm, but he flails as I try to pull him up.

'Leave me be.' He turns away from me.

'GET UP!' I yell, glancing around in case passers-by have noticed.

He mumbles something under his breath, sighs, and eases himself onto unsteady legs. 'Where are we going?'

Through gritted teeth I reply, 'To a café to get you

sobered up. Why have you started drinking again?'

'Dunno,' he mutters, stumbling along beside me.

Luckily, the nearby café is still open. I guide Michael to a chair and go and order us coffee. A mother at a nearby table stares at me, clasping her toddler close to her chest, so I toss her a faux smile to reassure her.

'You're an idiot,' I tell him when I return, shaking my head.

'You look nice. Where are you going?' he slurs, placing his booze carefully on the floor between his feet.

'Shit! Stay here.' I step away to text Flick, making the excuse of running late. When I return, the waitress has brought our order and Michael is hunched over the table sipping his drink.

'Can I get some water too?' I call over. She rolls her eyes but returns moments later with a filled bottle and two glasses.

Michael's head droops over his coffee, avoiding my glare. He finishes his drink and looks up at me through long eyelashes. 'Sorry ...'

'For what?'

'This.' He gestures to his empty cup.

'For coffee?' I pour a glass of water and push it towards him.

Without protest, he guzzles it in one go, sliding it back for a refill.

'What the hell happened?'

'I messed up,' he replies, eyes lowered. 'Lost my job.'

'Oh.'

'And the girl I'm into wants nothing to do with me.'

I close my eyes for a brief moment, digesting his words and trying to bury the guilt gnawing at my insides. 'I'm sorry—'

'Are you?' The furrow in his brow pierces any feeble defences I might have.

'You know I am,' I reply, slumping in my seat.

He nods. 'Well, thanks for rescuing me. You can go now.'

'I didn't rescue you,' I snap. 'Why would you say that?'

He shakes his head. 'Doesn't matter.'

My phone beeps, breaking the awkwardness now hanging like a storm cloud between us.

'Are you coming or what?' Flick's message reads.

'You'd better go—boyfriend's waiting.'

'I'm not leaving until you've sobered up.'

'There's no need.'

Anger bubbles and I glare up at him from my screen. 'You'd do the same.'

'Would I? Anyway, I need to go—'

I slam my phone on the table. 'Where?'

'I need to piss. Is that okay?'

'Fine.'

He gets up and wanders over to the back of the café. I watch him sway a little as he walks, eyeing his torso and ruffled hair.

By the time Michael returns, I have refilled his glass and disposed of his stash.

I push a menu towards him. 'Hungry?'

'No.'

'When did you last eat?'

'What do you care,' he says, rolling his eyes. 'Stop treating me like your pet project, will ya.'

'For God's sake!' I spit, fists clenching under the table. 'And for the record, I DO care!'

'There's no need. I'm not hungry and don't need a caretaker.'

I scowl at him. 'Fine, but the café's closing soon so drink up and we'll go for a walk to clear your head.'

'Yes miss!' He says, gulping the water, then gets up, his chair scraping across the café's decking.

I follow him out and we make our way towards a footpath running alongside the Swan river.

The sun is setting, casting a myriad of purples and burnt oranges across the sky, the ripples in the river twinkling in response.

We walk in silence for quite some time, reminding me so much of the times I spent with Jake in his rare sober moments, trying desperately to understand why he left home and holed up with junkies who wanted nothing more than to live hard, drink and shoot-up.

Trying to convince him that our parents would help. That *I* could help.

But he's not Jake, is he.

Eventually, Michael veers off towards a grassy bank, plopping himself down and sprawling out. He pats a spot next to him.

I sit beside him as daylight blinks a final goodbye.

'I love the water, how it ripples ...' Michael says, sounding wistful and more coherent. He pushes himself up into a sitting position. 'You okay? You look ... sad?'

I want to tell him to mind his own business, tell him that I should go, but Jake's image taunts me and words just spill out. 'My brother—Jake—he ... loved the water too.'

'Loved ...?' He leans towards me. 'What happened?'

'I couldn't save him.'

Michael listens without interruption, and when tears prick the corners of my eyes and trickle down my cheeks, he folds his arms tightly around me. I curl into his chest, sobbing.

My mobile pings, heaving me out of the moments of despair and I pull back from Michael, dabbing my eyes with the back on my hand.

I take my phone out of my bag and read a message from Flick. 'Are you still coming? We've already eaten and want to go clubbing.' But it's well past 9pm and truthfully, I'm in no fit state to party. Besides, being here with Michael has given me unexpected comfort. I don't want it to end. 'Don't feel good, so I'm going home,' I type back, and press send. Flick doesn't reply.

'I guess you'd better go,' Michael says, standing and reaching down to pull me up.

I gaze up at him, drawn in by his compassion and gentle smile. 'I ... I don't have to.'

'You don't,' he whispers, 'but you should.'

'I know, but—' and I reach up to his face and gently stroke his stubbled cheek.

He cups my hand, leaning in and softly kissing it. 'Go home, Clara. I'm a lost cause.'

I stare into eyes that hold an innate power to draw me in, desperation to cross the forbidden line building. I lunge towards him grabbing his head with my free hand and kiss him hard.

For a brief moment he is frozen, but then softens, his arm wrapping around my waist as a low groan emanates and he opens up to me.

'Clara—' he breathes between kisses. And I am lost.

~~~

'What time will you be home?' Dan's text, sent at 11:03pm, appears on my phone screen.

I glance at my watch—01:37am. *Shit!*

~~~

I pay the taxi driver and walk the green mile to the front door.

'Clara?' Dan's voice carries from inside.

Within seconds, the door's flung open.

'Where were you? Flick said you didn't make it,' he barks.

'Oh … I err … didn't make the meal. Met up with Tiff later.' I brush past him and into our bedroom.

'And you didn't think to call me?'

'I was really drunk … sorry.' I can't look at him. Can't let him see my guilt.

He walks away, swearing, as I head for the shower.

～～～

The following day at work I log into Facebook, my heart pounding as memories of the night before flit through my mind. And to my delight, there's a message from Michael.

'I'm sorry,' it says. 'Need to get myself sorted. Please don't hate me.'

I slump onto the laptop, sunk by an iceberg.

He's always sorry.

January 2016

Dan's Christmas present to me was a spa retreat in Bali, and it's been a long time coming. We are staying in Ubud amidst lush rainforests and lime green rice paddies and have spent our mornings sightseeing at the monkey sanctuary and Ubud Palace, and afternoons having massages, mud treatments and doing meditation. And as blissful as this all sounds, all is not well between us. We have cosy moments where I try to be present, but I know I am distancing myself from him and relishing in activities where we don't have to talk or be intimate. I'm sure he suspects that something is amiss, and it comes to a head over a degustation experience at the swanky Blanco restaurant on our last night in Bali.

Dan is quiet as we wait for our first course, periodically fidgeting and frowning as if he wants to say something but can't quite find the words. My discomfort increases exponentially.

Trying to lighten air hanging thick and heavy between us, I pipe up, 'This place is off the chart. How did you afford it?'

He proffers a weak smile and replies, 'I've been saving up.' It makes me feel worse.

The food arrives and Dan beckons the waiter closer, whispering in his ear.

'What was that about?' I ask.

'Oh … just ordering some more drinks,' Dan says, smoothing the napkin across his knee before tucking into the miniscule portion of Blue Swimmer crab on his plate and letting out an appreciative, 'mmm,' after a few bites.

I stare across at him, eyebrows arched as I scrutinise his face.

After the next three courses have been served and eaten, and still feeling as though there's plenty of room left in my stomach, Dan disappears to the bathroom affording me a moment to contemplate the strangeness of this evening. My gut twists as he returns, still sensing that something is not right, but rather than sitting back down, he stands at the side of me.

'Clara,' he says, 'there's something I need to say to you.'

I twist around to face him. 'Oh?'

He kneels down and I suddenly realise the tinkling music in the background has stopped.

'You are the love of my life, Clara. And I know we've had our ups and downs, but I can't imagine being with anyone else.' My heart drums in Prestissimo, anticipating what's coming next.

'Dan?' Panic wells and I glare at him.

He pulls a small box from his pocket and flips it open before me. 'Marry me, C? I love you and want to spend the rest of my life with you.'

My whole body stiffens, mouth agape, speechless as

I gaze down at the sparkling cluster ring with a fiery red and purple opal in the centre.

'Well?' He stares into me, eyebrows furrowed. 'C?'

Oh my God! What the hell?

Beads of sweat merge and trickle down his forehead, his eyes pleading me for an answer.

'Say something. Anything!'

As I look at him, noticing his face quickly souring to a frown, images of Michael flash before me creating a lava pool of guilt within. But I don't want to betray Dan, don't want to hurt him after all he's done for me, the answer popping out of me. 'Okay,' I nod.

'You will?' He breathes a sigh and beams. 'Jesus, C! You had me worried there for a minute.' And he grabs my hand and slides on the ring.

Shell-shocked, I look at the ring, then back at him, a big, fake smile plastered on my face.

What the hell have I done?

~~~

On the four-hour plane ride home, and despite my suggestions of there being no rush, Dan is talking about our wedding and wanting to set a date.

'I thought we could get married in November, the 22nd to be exact,' he says as I flick over the next page in my book.

'Huh? Why that date?'

'I just thought that it would be something nice to do after Jake's birthday.'

'That's a stupid idea,' I snap. 'Why the hell would you suggest that?'

'Don't bite my head off. It was just an idea,' he huffs.

I fold over the top corner of the page, close the book and rest it in my lap. 'Why are you so keen to get married so soon? We've got a lifetime together, remember.'

'Why are you so keen not to?' he throws back. 'Anybody would think you don't actually want to marry me.'

'You're being ridiculous. Let's talk about this when we get home.' I re-open my book hoping he'll take the hint.

'Fine,' he says releasing my hand and flicking on the TV screen.

~~~~~

'Let me see it,' Flick says, gushing, as I thrust my hand towards her and Tiff. They both takes turns to coo and paw the ring, giggling excitedly at the prospect of being maids of honour.

But after Tiff leaves, Flick and I remain at the café and order another round of coffees, and Flick says what I suspect she's been thinking for a while. 'You don't seem that excited about marrying Dan.' She sips her latte waiting for me to respond.

'Course I am,' I retort, 'it's just that it's all happened so fast. One minute we're saving for our own place, the next we're spending it all on a wedding.'

Flick nods, eyes narrowed. 'But there's something

else … something you're not telling me.' She eyes me with suspicion.

'No there isn't. I'm just needing time to get my head around it, that's all.'

'I know you, Clara, and I can see that things are not as peachy as you'd like me to believe. What's really going on?'

'Nothing! Well … maybe there is something, but it's not about me and Dan.'

'Work, then?'

Realising she's just given me a get-out clause, I nod. 'Yeah,' and sip my coffee.

'It'll come good,' she says, grabbing my hand across the table. 'Just needs time.' She smiles and squeezes my hand.

Yeah. Time is all it needs.

March 2016

Even after many protestations and arguments, Dan has worn me down and we are tying the knot on a beach at the Anantora Resort in Seminyak on 26th March. We have rented a huge villa to house us, our parents, and a select few friends. We have pissed off many relatives and friends with the plan—Dan's plan—and spent a good chunk of savings on this wedding package.

All the planning and arrangements have kept my mind off the actual day itself, so as the occasion draws near and everything becomes finalised, the panic really starts to set in.

My girls are with me as we shop for my wedding dress and their maid of honour dresses, mindful to keep them appropriate for the suffocating Bali humidity while still being elegant enough to pass off as bridal attire.

As I parade myself in front of them to a chorus of oohs and ahhs, my mind drifts to Jake as deep regrets and longings come into the furore. Jake would've been an usher, although part of me always dreamt of him and my Dad walking me down the aisle, or in this case, the fucking beach.

Not one for fluff and fancy, I settle on a backless chiffon dress in white with a lace body. Simple and elegant. The girls have chosen matching strapless maxi dresses in powder blue to match the shorts the groomsmen will be wearing. They all look stunning and happy with the choices, except Anna, who would much rather be in in something more casual.

~~~

My shoeless father slowly walks me along the sandy aisle and past rows of white chairs towards a square pagoda wrapped in white flowers and floaty material, housing a French-style table. The smartly dressed celebrant stands behind the table, Dan and his best man, Will, stand in front to the right-hand side. As cheesy Balinese music muffled by the sea breeze resounds, Dan turns to face me, beaming as I walk towards him.

My gut twists as I near, the enormity of the day finally sinking in, and I don't know if I feel elated or terrified.

Mum is already dabbing her eyes and Tiffany is sniffling behind me as I take my place by Dan's side and pass my small posy of daisies to Flick.

I gaze up at Dan and he winks at me, his face lit up by the setting sun. He really is handsome, and in that moment a breath escapes me as I take him in.

I do love this man.

~~~

After the nuptials, our small party is treated to a lavish buffet dinner in the resort restaurant overlooking the beach. We finish the night on the terrace, slow dancing to more popular tunes as stars twinkle into life. I am swept away by the romance of it all, and by the wonderful man I now call my husband.

We are spending the night in a luxurious Ocean Suite, complete with jacuzzi, and as Dan carries me across the threshold into our room, I notice our bed is laden with red roses, chocolates and a bottle of champagne. And after sipping bubbly in the bath, we make love as if we're getting to know each intimately other all over again.

April 2017

Dan and I have been married for just over a year and we've finally made the decision to buy a house, helped in part by my growing clientele and a promotion for Dan. Things are on the up and it should be an exciting time for us, but cracks have been forming for a while now, and I am slowly retreating into a shell, anticipating my next loss.

Work frustrates me. Although I have more clients and money is flowing well, I find the job emotionally draining, boring even, when I listen to some of the more benign woes my clients talk about.

My friends know I'm not happy, but I just feign a smile and say, 'it's fine. Just need to pull my head in,' when they ask the question.

I've also tried to check Michael's profile on Facebook several times, but it must be inactive. And as time goes by, more and more of my free time is spent out of Dan's way, holed up in the office trying to write, but only managing one or two lines before frustration kicks in and I flee to spend time with one of the girls. Dan says nothing, but I sense he's feeling the strain too. He is snappy and irritable when we disagree over something as trivial as what colour paint do we want in our new house, or should we get a dog? The cracks are becoming ravines.

Is this what married life is supposed to be like?

~~~~~~

One chilly morning on the way to work I pass by a familiar face at the train station.

'Hi,' Michael beams as we cross paths.

'Michael,' I breathe, stopped in my tracks.

'Been a while.'

I nod, still breathless.

'How are you?' His eyes sparkle and he looks smart.

'Good.' My voice wavers. 'You?'

'Sober,' he chuckles. 'And working.'

'That's great.' Uneasiness lingers and I look away, shuffling between feet. 'I'd better go. Gonna be late.' I toss him a smile. 'Nice to see you,' I say and walk away, the sound of my heart thumping resonating in my ears.

'Clara?'

I twist around to look at him. 'Michael—I'm married. I ... I can't do this anymore.'

He doesn't call after me.

~~~~~~

Several weeks have passed since my last encounter with Michael. Seeing him reignites the passion, the connection I feel with him, one I wish I could erase so I can focus on being present with the man who really loves me. But it's a struggle. Deep-down I know Dan and I are falling apart. When we are together, we are fighting; arguing about anything and everything, so-much-so that our house plans have been put on hold.

When I arrive home after a long and frankly boring day at work, Dan is in the garage sorting out boxes of knick-knacks on the shelves.

'Hey, what are you up to?' I ask as I walk up the driveway.

He doesn't stop to face me. 'Thought I'd sort through some of this stuff. Get organised for when we do finally get a house.'

'Oh right,' I reply. 'What do you want for dinner?'

'I had something at work so don't worry about me.'

'Fair enough,' and without another word, I head inside leaving Dan to his task.

I'm about to start putting together a salad for myself when my mobile pings with a message from Anna asking if me and the girls want to come around to her place because she has news.

I pop my head around the garage door. 'Anna's invited me and the girls over. You don't mind if I head out for a bit?'

He looks up and rolls his eyes. 'Like I have a choice?'

'Don't be like that!' I snap, and don't wait for his response as I head inside and grab my bag and car keys.

~~~

Stella, back from studying in the UK, is the last one to arrive as Anna pours more glasses of wine and we settle on the sofas for a catch-up.

'So what's the news?' Tiff pipes up, glugging back

her wine.

Anna's eyes light up. 'There's two bits,' she grins. 'Firstly, you are now looking at the Head of Marketing for the City of Perth—'

We all whoop and cheer, clinking our glasses in recognition of a well-deserved promotion.

'And secondly, Mia and I are getting married!'

After gasps of delight and more clinking, Flick asks, 'is that legal yet?'

'Not yet. But hopefully soon.'

'That's fantastic news!' I reach over and squeeze Anna, whose eyes are watery with tears. But all-at-once, my jubilation sours as thoughts of mine and Dan's less-than-happy marriage come to mind. I only hope Anna has much better luck. Surely some relationships are meant to last.

August 2017

Dan's face flushes crimson as I look up at him through tear-drenched eyes.

'This is bullshit, Clara. You'd rather spend time with your friends than me!'

We have been fighting for hours, all because I wanted to go to the movies with Flick, and now I've run out of excuses.

'I'm sorry,' I reply. 'I never meant for it to get like this.'

'Really?' he replies, eyes fiery.

'I love you, but it—it isn't working. I'm so sorry ...'

He punches the wall, roaring as plaster and fist collide.

I slope away to the bedroom as he whispers, 'I love you too,' and start packing.

~~~

The winter chill has set in and I hurry to the station to catch the train home to my new rental apartment that doesn't yet feel like home and has my failings written all over it.

As I walk along the overpass, a man slumped against the wall mutters something incomprehensible. I glance down at him—wrapped up in an old parka jacket, a straggly beard covering his mouth and chin, and his face ruddy from the cold.

'Clara?' He smiles, and I notice a cracked front tooth and wisps of grey in his beard.

'Michael?' It takes a moment for recognition to fully kick in. 'What are you doing here?'

He clambers up until we are face-to-face. 'Long story. Wanna buy me a coffee?' No protests, no bottle of booze with him this time.

We find a café outside of the station and sit inside at a table away from everyone else, heads periodically turning and faces glaring.

'What's going on?' I ask softly.

'Lost my job again.'

'Drink?'

He nods, head dropping.

'Michael ...' I reach over and squeeze his hand.

He looks up, tears pooling in his eyes. 'They've given up on me.'

'Who?'

'Everyone. I fucked up too many times.' He covers his face and sobs.

'I'm so sorry ...'

~~~

I'm preparing dinner when the kitchen door creaks open. A freshly groomed Michael appears wearing only a bath towel. His torso is lean, his skin sallow, but unleashed desire courses through me.

After eating, we spend the night talking, touching, and making love, deepening this strange long-held connection between us.

The Universe has given me another shot, only this time, I won't fail.

~~~

The note on my bedside table reads, 'I'm sorry. I love you.'

Michael has gone.

December 2017

As I flick through the local rag, my eyes fall on a large notice in 'Obituaries':

'Michael Joseph Moran, beloved son. Died 22 November 2017 aged 34.

Funeral to be held at Immaculate Heart of Mary,

Scarborough on 13th December 2017 at 2pm.'

My cup smashes into tiny pieces on the floor.

I feel numb and barely register the priest's words or the dedications from friends and family sparsely occupying the pews. But the sobs of Michael's nearest and dearest echo around the cold, cavernous church. As the service ends and the congregation leaves, I dutifully make my way to the entrance towards an elderly couple who I believe are Michael's parents.

'I'm so sorry ...' I offer, shaking the man's hand. 'I'm Clara. I ... I worked with Michael at the prison.'

The woman, her puffy eyes widening, reaches into her handbag. 'This must be for you, then,' she says, pushing a crumpled envelope towards me.

I take hold of it, staring at my name on the front. 'Um ... thanks,' I mumble, and stash it in my bag.

I quick step out of the churchyard desperate to contain whatever is threatening to burst out as my head starts to spin like an errant Catherine wheel.

I wish Jake were here to hold me and tell me it'll all be okay. But he's gone too, nothing but a weathered headstone on a patchy grass bed to identify him. I can't bear to see the same for Michael.

So, I walk the short distance to the Church on the Esplanade and make my way to Jake's grave.

The last book I left him for his birthday is still there, next to pots of decayed flowers. I pick it up and stash it in my bag and set about removing the flowers. I have to keep busy or I know I'll fall, but as I wipe down the headstone and tidy up the grave, one thought goes on repeat, 'Why do they always leave me, Jake? Why?'

~~~

All rational thought has left. I find myself standing atop a sand dune on Scarborough beach. How did I get here? The empty bottle of vodka, still wrapped in a brown paper bag, is in my hand. Staring out towards the place Jake lost his life, images of him, then of Michael lying face-down in the wash play like horror movies in my mind. The sea beckons me.

As if in a trance, I drop my bag and kick off my shoes onto the sandy shore about three feet from the tide mark and tiptoe, still fully clothed, into the Indian Ocean, wading until the water reaches my neck.

I can't do this anymore—can't face another loss, so I give in, ready for the sea to claim me as tears stream down my face. A king wave surges over my head, swallowing me whole and tossing me around until the undercurrent grabs me in its unforgiving pull ...

~~~

Water fizzes up my nose and I gasp back to life, spluttering.

The sea has spat me out and the wash has carried me back up the shore to safety.

Sodden and covered in sand, I stumble back up the beach to where I left my bag and sit, panting and trembling from the icy clothes clinging to my flesh.

With trembling fingers, I pull the envelope given to me by Michael's mother out of my bag, unfold the letter inside and read it:

> *'Dear Clara,*
>
> *Leaving you sleeping that morning was the hardest thing I've ever done. I wanted to come back to you so many times, but I just couldn't live with myself if I let you waste your life on me.*
>
> *I had so many opportunities to quit the booze, but guess I was beyond saving. Your brother and me—well, we had choices, and we had people who loved us enough to keep trying, but we still took the easy way out.*
>
> *I've messed up so many times and now my chances have run out. Guess I've got the ending to my story now, eh.*
>
> *It's been an adventure for us, though, hasn't it, and maybe one day you can write about it for me, only with a much happier ending.*

I just want you to know that I'm so glad to have known you, Clara. And whatever you may think, you did save me in many ways, if only I could've saved myself before it was too late.

Love always,

Michael.'

'I love you too,' I whisper, and the dam wall holding back the true force of my grief for Jake and Michael finally erupts as I double over and open the flood gates.

~~~

Darkness falls as I arrive home, my head lighter, my heart steadied, as if the cage I'd constructed to harbour my losses has been thrust open and washed clean.

After showering and grabbing a bite to eat, I make myself a coffee, flip open my laptop and begin typing with a renewed passion:

'Jake Reid: poster boy of addiction.'

I don't stop until the early hours, driven by the desire to put into words what has evaded me for so long. Maybe now I can finally understand.

The End

About the Author

Lisa is a mum, wife, former IT project leader and ex-crisis counsellor who now directs Dragonfly Publishing after a two-year stint as co-director of Footprints Publishing Pty Ltd.

She was previously on the Katharine Susannah Prichard (KSP) Writers' Centre Board of Management and the Executive Officer of their publishing service, Wild Weeds Press. She has facilitated a writing group at the centre and hosted creative writing and self-publishing workshops.

Lisa is drawn to penning stories about life and loss, with a dash of love sometimes thrown in for good measure.

When not writing or loitering around the Perth Hills, Lisa enjoys reading, travelling, music and more wine thank is good for her.

Book news can be found on Lisa's website:

www.lisawolstenholme.com or on Facebook, Instagram and Twitter.

Other Books by the Author

The Sunrise Girl – contemporary women's fiction novel

– Dragonfly Publishing, Dec 2021

For the Love of Dogs – romance novelette

- Gumnut Press, Sep 2021

Pawprints of Love – romance anthology

- Gumnut Press, May, 2020

When Love Breaks Down – romance novelette

- Serenity Press, Jul 2020

Destination Romance – romance anthology

- Serenity Press, Dec 2019

Passages – contemporary women's fiction anthology

- Serenity Press, Dec 2019

All Lisa's books can be purchased from major online booksellers.

Printed in Australia
AUHW02083523122
372923AU00043B/222